Sue MacKay lives with her husband in New Zealand's beautiful Marlborough Sounds, with the water on her doorstep and the birds and the trees at her back door. It is the perfect setting to indulge her passions of entertaining friends by cooking them sumptuous meals, drinking fabulous wine, going for hill walks or kayaking around the bay—and, of course, writing stories.

Also by Sue MacKay

The Italian Surgeon's Secret Baby
Redeeming Her Brooding Surgeon
Taking a Chance on the Single Dad
The Nurse's Twin Surprise

**London Hospital Midwives
collection**

Cinderella and the Surgeon
by Scarlet Wilson
Miracle Baby for the Midwife
by Tina Beckett
Reunited by Their Secret Daughter
by Emily Forbes
A Fling to Steal Her Heart

Available now

Discover more at millsandboon.co.uk.

A FLING
TO STEAL
HER HEART

SUE MacKAY

MILLS & BOON

First published in Great Britain 2020
by Mills & Boon, an imprint of HarperCollins*Publishers*
1 London Bridge Street, London, SE1 9GF

Large Print edition 2020

© 2020 Sue MacKay

ISBN: 978-0-263-08581-5

MIX
Paper from
responsible sources
FSC® C007454

This book is produced from independently certified
FSC™ paper to ensure responsible forest management. For
more information visit www.harpercollins.co.uk/green.

Printed and bound in Great Britain
by CPI Group (UK) Ltd, Croydon, CR0 4YY

CHAPTER ONE

'ARE YOU CERTAIN you aren't still in love with him?'

'Couldn't be more certain.'

Isabella Nicholson held back on saying more. Admitting the truth that she doubted she'd really loved her ex enough in the first place would be embarrassing, even if Raphael Dubois was her best friend.

Best as in she'd usually tell him everything, whenever the urge took her, even in the early hours of Sunday morning, which it was right now. Four a.m. here in Wellington, four p.m. Saturday in London, where Raphael worked at his dream job in obstetrics and gynaecology at the Queen Victoria Hospital.

Wait a minute. He'd texted to see if *she* was awake, and knowing she currently suffered insomnia it was a no-brainer.

'Hey, why did you call? Not to ask about Darren, surely?'

'Izzy, is that the absolute truth or are you afraid of the answer?'

Typical. The man never missed a beat when it came to asking the hard questions, whether of her or his patients. Yet he always ignored *her* questions whenever it suited him.

Two could play that game. Though she'd try once more to shut him down. 'Don't I always tell you the truth?' Minus some niggling details in this instance.

'You're good at leaving out the specifics when it suits,' he confirmed, chuckling so she knew he was letting go the subject of her failed marriage.

'So what brings you to call in the middle of Saturday afternoon? I'd have thought you'd be at a rugby game with the guys.' One of them had found the niche they were looking for—and it wasn't her. Two years ago she'd returned home to New Zealand with her new husband, full of hope and excitement based around Darren's promises for what lay ahead, and with the intention of finally stopping in one place and surrounding herself with family and friends. Instead, twelve months later, her marriage had crashed badly, leaving her dreams up in the air. The friends had been all his, and her parents were always busy with their own lives. Since then she'd gone back to what she was good at—moving around the world from job to country to anywhere enticing, only for a lot shorter periods than previously. A fortnight ago she'd finished a volunteers' job in Cambodia and returned to visit her parents while deciding where next. Only she couldn't bring herself to go just anywhere this time.

Find something more permanent kept popping into her head. *Go solo on that dream of settling down.*

'I've been delivering triplets,' Rafe replied. He'd settled in London, been there nearly three years, bought a house, was keeping some distance from his claustrophobic family at home in Avignon as he grappled with his own demons. He seemed content in a quiet way, which was not the Raphael she'd known most of her life.

Please be her turn next. Even if it meant remaining single, which wasn't so bad. She was used to it. Nursing and midwifery jobs were fairly easy to come by, but after a childhood of moving around with her parents in the Foreign Service she'd hankered after settling back in New Zealand for ever when she'd married. Maybe that's where she'd gone wrong, put too much emphasis on where she lived and not who with. So here she was, minus the husband, ignoring the hole inside that needed filling with something unrecognisable, and which she suspected had to do with love. 'Triplets. Hard to imagine how parents cope with that many babies all at once.'

'This couple would've been grateful for quads if it meant becoming parents.' His voice fell into sentimental mode. 'You should see these little guys. So cute, looking tiny in their incubators hooked up to monitors, giving their parents heart failure already.'

'But they'll be fine, right?' He'd hate for anything to go wrong. When a baby in his care had difficulties that couldn't be fixed he'd get upset for days, distraught for the parents, blaming himself while knowing it wasn't his fault. She'd never been able to find out what was behind his extreme reaction that had only started over the last few years. Seemed they both kept secrets from each other.

'For triplets they're in good shape, though one of them is smaller than his brothers so I'll be keeping a closer eye on him. They made it to thirty-four weeks' gestation before the Caesarean, which means everything's on their side. The parents had fertility issues so we did artificial insemination and, *voilà*, the best of results.' Raphael's accent thickened when he became emotional.

'Great outcome for all of you.' Because he would've been almost as invested as the expectant parents. 'You should go out and celebrate.'

'I'm meeting up with a couple of the guys and their better halves as soon as I've talked with you. What did you get up to last night?'

Huh? Her social life had never been of much interest to him before. There again, recently he had taken to expressing concern about how she was coping with getting over Darren. Worried she'd go back to the cheat?

'I went out for a meal and a couple of drinks at the local with a neighbour.' She hadn't stayed out late, preferring to head back to her parents' place rather than being eyed up by men obviously wanting one thing only.

Getting old, girl.

Or jaded.

'Beats staying inside the four walls feeling sorry for yourself.'

Again, huh? What was this all about? 'That's harsh, Rafe.' She preferred it when Raphael went all sentimental over the babies he delivered, not digging deeper into her messed-up life. 'I'll say it one more time. I do not love Darren. Any feelings I had for him died when I found Gaylene Abernethy's naked body wrapped around him in our bed.' If only it was that easy: blame Darren for everything and feel superior. But it wasn't. She'd taken his promises about their life together at face value, colouring in the gaps with what she wanted and not seeing that he'd never aspired to the same. Though the affairs were a different story. Her husband had gone too far there.

'That's positive. I had to ask.' That couldn't be relief in Raphael's voice. Then again, why not? The two men had never got on, were summer to winter.

'Sure you did.'

Naturally he hadn't finished. 'Love doesn't always stop the moment there's a reason to.' He spoke from firsthand experience. Was that what this was about? Would he finally tell her what had happened six years ago when his heart was torn out of his chest?

'I did love Darren, though not as much as I should've if I was committing to "until death us do part."'

'Does anyone say that any more? What if you both lived till you were ninety-five? That's a lot of marriage. At fifty who's the same person they were at thirty, let alone in their nineties?' asked the guy who'd signed up for ever with Cassie, only to get the boot within two years. Failed marriages were another thing they had in common.

'Typical of you to come up with that question.' If she fed him a little bit more about her relationship would he let it go? Not likely. This was Rafe. Neither did admitting how she'd failed come easily. She'd made a mistake marrying Darren. His promises of buying a house and having children didn't eventuate. Instead the parties, going to the rugby games with the mates and leaving her behind, the late nights at the office not working—found that out later—the weekends away with the boys… None of it ever stopped, actually became more intense, as though he was afraid to face what he'd agreed to do with her. She'd got more morose and by the time their first wedding anniversary came around she was blaming him for everything that went wrong in her life. Not accepting that she'd rushed in on those promises without asking herself if she really loved Darren as much as she'd believed. 'I'm fine. I made a mistake, and now I've put it behind me.'

'As long as you're sure,' Raphael muttered. 'I don't want you regretting leaving him further down the track.'

'Drop it, Rafe. We are not getting back together. It's over.' How many times did she have to say it?

'Right. Tell me about Phnom Penh, then. What made you stay on an extra month?'

She'd rather talk about her ex. 'A tragic case that I got too close to.'

'We're not meant to do that, Izzy.'

Tell her something she didn't know. 'It's different over there. When someone's sick or seriously injured the whole family's involved, from great-gran to baby brother, and I got swept up in it all.' To the point where she'd put the brakes on racing around chasing happiness while she thought about what she really wanted for the future. 'Can we change the subject?'

'Fine. So what's next? A summer at the Antarctic with the New Zealand science contingent? Or a month on one of the charity ships in Africa?'

There seemed to be another question behind Raphael's queries, but Isabella couldn't hear what it was. Strange, given how well they knew each other—apart from those secrets. 'Come on. I'm not that restless.'

Though the past year said otherwise. Auckland, Melbourne, Cambodia. Maybe she was more like her parents than she cared to admit, and therefore she was never going to find that permanent happy place. Nothing wrong with Mum and Dad's thirty-two-year marriage despite rarely stopping in one place for more than three years at a time though. They just shouldn't have brought her into the mix. 'I spent six years in Wellington training and working as a nurse. Four more in London doing midwifery before—'

'*Oui*, I get it. But right now you'll be overthinking what you're going to do next. Stay in Wellington, move to Africa or America.' He paused. Then on a deep breath, he continued. 'With your attitude about failing, this breakup will still be winding you into a tight ball of conjecture. "Where shall I live? What's the next project to undertake? Am I more Kiwi or English?"' He sighed, then said, 'Tell me I'm wrong, Izzy.'

She couldn't. That was exactly who she was. Except that family in Cambodia had changed her in some indefinable way. But she wasn't ready to talk about it yet. Might never be. Isabella stretched the length of her bed, and tucked the thick woollen duvet around herself. 'You'll be pleased to know I can't imagine being stuck on an iceberg for months on end having to rely on in-depth conversations with penguins.' She pulled her pillow down around her neck. Autumn had thrown a curve ball today, sending a reminder of what winter would have in store in a few weeks.

'Penguins are probably more interesting than half the people you get to meet every day.' His laughter was usually infectious, but tonight it was sounding a little tired, fed up even.

'Something wrong at your end of the world?'

'No more than the usual. We're short-staffed and it seems every female in London over twenty is pregnant at the moment.'

'What about life outside the Queen Victoria? Love, life, laughter, those things?' Raphael was one of the most good-looking men she knew. Women fawned over him, fell in love with him without him having said *bonjour*. Yet, since Cassie, he'd not had one serious relationship, preferring the love 'em and leave 'em approach to relationships—when he found time for one. At least he didn't promise anything else and always warned the women he wasn't looking for a partner. In fact, he was so kind and careful about his approach they all still thought he was wonderful long after he'd said *au revoir.*

'Don't know what you're talking about.' At least his laughter was genuine now. 'Haven't got time for much than work and study.'

'That sounds as pathetic as my life right now.' What a scintillating pair they made.

'You think?' Raphael took a long, slow breath. 'Crunch time, huh, Midwife Nicholson? For you, not me,' he clarified.

'You sure about that?' she grumped, hating him for making her face up to what was bothering her.

'It's not me lying awake for hours every night trying to put the pieces of the puzzle back together.'

'You're right, and don't you dare gloat,' she added in a hurry. 'I do have some decisions to make.'

'Starting with?'

That was the problem. She didn't know where to start. 'Where to live?'

'What's wrong with where you are?' Straight to the point, as always.

'If I'm staying here I need to buy a property and get stuck in making it mine.' Isabella sighed. It was the truth, just not all of it. Try again. 'Funny how I always thought of Wellington as home and yet it doesn't feel like that.'

'You haven't exactly been happy there in the past. We all need some place to call home, but it doesn't mean we have to settle there if we're not getting what we require from it. Like me and Avignon.'

Yeah, where he got too much of what he wanted. 'Now there's an interesting city.' The ancient wall surrounding the city centre, the old fort on the other side of the river, the famous Pont d'Avignon. The history had drawn her, made her yearn to belong somewhere, to feel a part of something—and so when Darren came along she'd moved back to Wellington with him. Except now she'd probably leave again. Something was missing. With the city? Or inside her? 'I think I want to get back to friends who *know* me and where I've come from.' Maybe even *where* she was headed.

Raphael should understand. They'd met on trips with their respective schools to a ski field in the Swiss Alps. Out of control on a snow board, she'd crashed into him, and nursing bruises over hot chocolate in the café they'd instantly bonded. His father worked in a bank in Geneva while her dad was working at the New Zealand consulate in the same city. She'd been used to making friends quickly, aware how fast three years passed when she'd have to move and start all over again. Raphael had been homesick for his grandmother and cousins back in Avignon, and resented his parents for taking him away from them all. She'd wanted her parents to return home and stop moving. Instead, when her mother obtained a position in an international accounting company that had her travelling a lot, Isabella had been sent to boarding school in England, leaving her feeling unconnected, abandoned. Even when she returned to the family fold, that disconnect remained. She'd done too much growing up in the interim and had changed for ever.

Despite being two years older than her, Raphael had gone out of his way to keep in touch, and they had remained close, despite living in different countries for most of their friendship. She'd briefly worked with him once in Tours, which had been great. Since then? Modern communications systems were the best thing to ever be invented.

Raphael asked, 'You're still coming over here for Carly's wedding, right?'

'Wouldn't miss it for anything. It was bad enough not making it to Esther and Harry's.' She'd been supposed to fly to London for that, but when the Medical Volunteers Charity asked her to stay on another month because the traumatised Khy family she'd been working closely with still needed her there as stability, she hadn't been able to say no. They'd needed her, and she'd wanted to be needed. Still did. 'Flights are booked.'

'Why not make it a one-way trip? Your

girlfriends from midwifery training days are here and all working in the Queen Victoria, although for how long is anyone's guess with all these weddings going down. Then there's *moi*.'

Her laugh was brittle. 'You make it sound so easy.' It was. With an English mother getting a work visa for the UK was straightforward. But did she want to go there and be watched over like she was going to come out in a rash for being on her own again? Or questioned about every move she made? Every decision she arrived at? Because Raphael had changed. Since she'd left Darren, come to think of it. He was always questioning what she did, the jobs she chose, the countries they were in. No way did she want put up with any more of that, and living on his back doorstep wouldn't help. At least she wouldn't be *in* his house.

He continued in a coaxing voice. 'Okay, why I really rang. There is a nurse's position coming up on my ward if you're interested. With your midwifery qualifications as well as nursing you're ideal for the job. The girl who's leaving hasn't told anyone other than me yet, and she's agreed to keep quiet till I talk to you. What do you think?'

'How soon would I have to start?' She was stalling, not feeling the excitement that usually stirred when she had an offer on the table to do something new. Weighing up the pros and cons? Unlike her.

'Jasmine wants to be gone within three weeks. Something about a boyfriend in Canada and a road trip they've been planning to do over summer.'

Did she want to return to London? As in *really* want to? Or should she be staying put, making more of an effort to integrate into Wellington and stop blaming Darren for feeling confused? Making this the home base she'd always wanted?

'And...ta da, the best bit.' He paused for effect. Typical Raphael. 'Don't forget who's the charge obstetrician on the ward. Your call, but remember, we work well together.'

That they did. Working as a midwife for those few months in Tours just after she'd finished her midwifery training had been

the best job she'd ever had; having her clos-
est friend in the same hospital added to the
pluses. He'd shown her the French lifestyle,
taken her to Avignon to meet his maternal
grandmother and his cousins, tripped all over
the country on their days off to show her cas-
tles, cities, mountains. Then he'd taken up
his current position in London, and she'd met
Darren in France while watching a rugby
game between the All Blacks and Les Bleus,
and the rest was history. A rocky, sorry history, but what didn't kill her was going to
make her stronger. Just not certain when. Not
to mention how persuasive Raphael could be
when he put his mind to it. 'You know what?'

'You're on your way.'

'I might be.'

'Hello? Where's strong, do-it-her-way-or-
bust Isabella gone? You're coming or you're
not. Which, Izzy?'

She had to make her mind up now? Why
not? Raphael was right. She'd always approached life head-on, didn't usually waste
time dithering over decisions, and accepted
that when she'd got it wrong it was part of

the gamble. Her marriage failure had set her off kilter, made her worry and fuss too much about getting things right or wrong, made her wary of trusting people. Then watching the closeness of the Khys as they struggled to keep their son alive and how they coped after it all went wrong had blitzed her completely.

'Izzy?'

If taking up a new position back in the city where her nursing friends and Raphael lived turned out to be a mistake, then she'd survive. If Rafe became too bossy she'd tell him what to do with that. But at least they were all there, the people who mattered the most to her. 'Got to go. Have to pack my bag.'

CHAPTER TWO

TWO WEEKS LATER, as Raphael paced the arrivals hall at Heathrow, Isabella's text pinged on his phone.

Landed.

About time. Something settled in his gut. Relief? No, this sensation felt stronger, not that he recognised it, but it did make him wary and happy all in one hit. He'd felt this way when Izzy said she was coming to London. His fingers flew over his phone.

I'm waiting in arrivals hall.

The flight was an hour late. Serve him right for getting here early, but he'd been ready to pick up Izzy since crawling out of bed first light that morning. Not even doing a round of his patients and checking on the triplets had quelled the need to get to Heathrow on time, which in his book meant early. Very early. He'd given his regular visit to the market a miss, cursed the traffic holdups all the way to the airport and ranted at the arrivals notice board every time it brought up a new flight arrival that wasn't Izzy's. Damn it, he even checked his phone app every time to make sure the board and the app were on the same page. *Oui*, of course they were. But this hanging around for Isabella was doing his head in.

He couldn't wait to see her. It seemed ages since she'd married Darren, who in his book was a complete idiot, and left London for what she euphemistically—in his mind, desperately—called home. It had been as though she'd been on a mission to prove something to herself, and she hadn't told him what it was, which worried him. Yet when Isabella suggested he pay them a visit in Wellington during his leave last year he'd pleaded prior commitments so as to avoid her husband. Unfair, but he and Darren had never seen eye to eye about anything, and especially about the woman they both cared about. Her husband could not get his head around the fact that Raphael and Isabella were close friends, not lovers and never had been, and he kept making digs about how she was *his*. Yeah, right. Look where that had got the guy. Single again, and still missing the whole point about commitment.

His phone pinged again.

Bring a trailer?

You've brought that much gear?

Yep.

Really? Isabella travelled light. Something she'd learned as a Foreign Service brat. While her parents had a container-load of gear follow them wherever they went, Izzy never packed much at all, said carrying only her regular gear around kept her grounded in reality. Did this mean she'd come to London with the idea of staying long term?

Calmes-toi.

There was long term and then there was Izzy's ingrained version of staying put. They did not match. There'd been nothing to stop her settling in London permanently last time she lived here. But he wasn't being fair. She had decided to stay here and then along came the husband offering all sorts of carrots in Wellington. She'd always had a thing about returning to the city where she'd been born and partially brought up in, so Darren's promises raised her hopes of a life there. The failure of said marriage seemed to have screwed with that idea, and stalled her about making any serious decisions over what to do next. Odd, because Isabella was no stranger to being strong and getting what she wanted. But on the other side of that argument, she *didn't* always know exactly what she wanted. Hence fast-track midwifery training.

He texted back.

Great.

It was, actually. Could be she'd finally figured out what she was looking for. Given half a chance he'd go back to Avignon and the family tomorrow. But it wasn't happening any time soon. He'd return there only when he'd got over the guilt for the way Cassie had treated his nearest and dearest. And stopped feeling angry for the cruel blow she'd hit him with. His son, his parents' only grandson, dead at eight days from SIDS, and he hadn't even known he was a father. The pregnancy one more of Cassie's ways of paying him back for not falling into line with all her outrageous demands.

The doors from the other side swished open as a small group of people towing cases on wheels came through. Swallowing the familiar bitterness and hauling his concentration to what was important today, Raphael craned his neck trying to see around them. No sign of Isabella. Nothing on his phone. 'Come on. Where are you?' he ground out. No doubt dealing with the inevitable questions from immigration. He'd take another turn of the hall to fill in some minutes.

Except Raphael remained glued to the spot, his eyes never leaving the doors now that his phone had gone quiet. Hopefully that meant she'd soon burst through the doors like the hurricane she could be. Not that she sounded as revved up these days whenever he talked to her. Her ex had dealt some harsh blows to her confidence. Though there could be more to it than Izzy was telling him.

The doors opened again and more exhausted people spilled through, followed by a laden trolley being pushed by... 'Raphael.' The shout was accompanied by a small body hurtling through the crowd, aimed directly for him.

'Izzy.'

Oof. *Oui*. Definitely tornado.

His lungs huffed out every last molecule of oxygen they were holding as Isabella plastered herself against him. His arms wound around her like they never intended letting go. She smelt of travel and tiredness and excitement and—

Mais oui, Isabella. Soft, tough.

Careful. Friends, nothing else.

'Hello, Rafe. Good to see you.'

The relief expanded. Isabella *was* here. Izzy. He inhaled deeper, hugged harder and kissed her on both cheeks French style.

Friendly style. Then, without letting go of her, he leaned back to gaze down at her fine features with dark shadows staining her upper cheeks. There was strain in her eyes, negating her usual go-get-'em attitude. Anger lodged behind his ribs. This was Darren's fault. The man had hurt her. But apparently it took two to tango, so had Isabella done something wrong too? He'd leave off the big questions until she'd got some sleep and was looking more like her normal self. Since the flat she'd arranged had fallen through she was staying with him for a little while—until they had their first row at least. Something not uncommon between them. 'Great to see you, *mon amie.*'

The familiar cheeky twinkle was back in her gaze, though the corners of her mouth were still drawn. 'You see me every other week.'

He relaxed enough to go with the change. 'Usually your chin is huge and your eyes somewhere above the screen. This way I get to see you properly. I can read your expressions,' he added to wind her up for the hell of it. Because that's how they'd always been with each other, and until now he hadn't realised how important it was. It kept him on track, especially at the times Cassie's betrayal got to him too much. He hadn't shared the details, but Izzy had always been at the end of a phone. They knew each other better than anyone, and had often relied on that to get through the upheavals life threw at them, yet there'd been apprehension in his veins since Isabella had agreed to come to London and take up the job he'd suggested. He didn't understand his apprehension, unless it was to do with the uncomfortable, almost painful, feeling that overcame him at her marriage ceremony where he'd stood beside her as she said her vows to Darren. A sense that he'd found out something important when it was too late.

'Next time I'll focus the camera on my slipper-covered feet.'

'Not the ones the neighbour's dog chewed.' Next time. Reality check. This wasn't a long-term move. Was that disappointment rapping his knuckles? And if so, why? He was used to her coming and going as it suited, or, when they were young, as her parents had decreed. Could be that his need to see her happy wasn't going to be satisfied. Could also be that his hope of spending more time with her wasn't going to be fulfilled. He looked around. 'We'd better rescue that trolley before someone crashes into it and the bags topple off.' This was going to be interesting. His car wasn't made for organising a complete house move. 'Did you leave anything behind?'

Her tight laugh had him wondering just what was going on. 'This is only the beginning. I'm shipping more belongings across. The container's due to arrive sometime in May.'

Raphael dived right in. 'So you're looking for somewhere to unpack properly? As in lock, stock and clothes?' This was nothing like her usual style of one backpack and the laptop.

Her laughter died. 'Don't be so shocked. Just because it didn't work in Wellington doesn't mean it won't here with all my friends around me.'

He reached for her, needing to hug a smile

back onto her face. 'You're right, and I'm one of them.'

'I hope so,' she murmured against his chest before pulling away, still without a smile. She'd never doubted him before. But before he could question her, she continued. 'There's a couple of pieces of furniture, some kitchenware and lots of books coming.'

He stared at her, a knot of unease tightening in his belly. She was serious about this move. He was thrilled for her, and him, and would help make it work, but… But he'd have to be careful about keeping his distance. Risking their friendship was not happening over some out of kilter emotions he'd felt on and off since her marriage. 'Truly?'

She nodded, her mouth twisted into a wry smile. 'Truly.' A sigh trickled over her lips. 'I'll add to them as soon as I find my own place.'

'Your own place?' The relief should be flooding in. It wasn't.

'A place to rent for a start.'

He sighed. *Stop being disgruntled.* His friend was back in town. Someone to talk the talk with, have a beer at the pub or take a ride out in the countryside. One day at a time and see how they went getting back to that easy relationship they'd always shared until she'd got married.

It goes back further than that, mon ami. *You've never shared much about your time with Cassie. Or the devastation she caused.*

'Thanks for putting a roof over my head until I find somewhere.'

'It'll be better than squatting under London Bridge.' Suddenly there was a bounce in his step. He'd been looking forward to this moment, and now Izzy was here. Right beside him. Recently his life had become all about work, and very little play. All too often he cancelled going to rugby with the guys, the only excuse being his patients needed him. But he needed to be more rounded, balance his lifestyle. Izzy was good at shaking him up, would take no nonsense about how he was a doctor before all else. Well, he was, but she always reckoned that didn't mean his work should fill twenty-four hours every day of the week. 'Let's get out of here.'

'Let's.' Isabella smothered a yawn with her hand. 'That was one hell of a trip. Crying babies, and an enormous man in the seat next to me who kept falling asleep and sprawling in every direction, mostly mine.'

'Sounds fairly normal.' Long-haul flights were hell on wings.

'One day I'm going to fly first class just to see what it's like. I did get some sleep though, which is a change. Probably because I had so little in the nights leading up to getting on the plane.'

'You done anything about that insomnia?'

Untidy auburn hair flicked across her shoulders as she shook her head. 'What's the point? I've tried everything except sleeping pills and I'm never resorting to them. Seen too many patients who've become addicted, and then any gains in the sleep department are lost. Besides, I'm used to getting by on a couple of hours at a time.'

This had gone on for almost as long as he'd known her, sometimes minor sleep deprivation, sometimes quite major, and in recent years it had cranked up a few more notches.

Guess a person could get used to anything given enough time, though it wasn't good for her. 'Still, I think you should see one of my colleagues. He's good at helping people get to the bottom of what's causing the problem and might even be able to give you some practical advice.'

'Let me get unpacked before you start organising my life.' Isabella gave him a lopsided smile, with a warning behind it. 'Okay, what've you got planned for tonight?'

Whatever she was trying to tell him, he'd leave it for now. 'Running three laps of the neighbourhood before digging up the back garden and putting in some plants.'

'Cool. Nothing for me to worry about. I can sit down and watch a movie on my phone, dial out for pizza.'

Raphael laughed, and it was like pushing Play on an old CD player, bringing back memories of fun times when his heart hadn't been ripped out of his chest. He halted the trolley to sling an arm over Isabella's shoulders and hug her against him again. 'You're on to it.' This was more like it. Cheeky Izzy not taking any of his nonsense seriously. It was one of the things he missed the most. Not even the overloaded, heavy trolley could put a dent in the sense of fun ahead now spreading through him. A familiar feeling he'd known the very first time they'd met, stronger than the pain in his thigh where her snowboard had struck hard. She'd been embarrassed at losing control, and tried blaming him for being in the way. They'd argued and laughed and shared hot chocolates and swapped phone numbers, and afterwards met up every weekend in Geneva when they could get away from school activities. 'I've missed you.' It hadn't been so easy to have two-hour conversations when there was a husband in the background, and he'd been very aware of how he might've felt if the situation had been reversed. He mightn't have liked Darren, but he understood the boundaries. And afterwards, Izzy had been a bit withdrawn with him.

'Same.'

'I would've headed down under for a week this past year to support you, cheer you up, get you back on track, but you were never there.' Her phone calls over the last twelve months had been quiet, and filled with sadness and, at times, something like despair that she'd never explained.

Again those auburn locks swished back and forth across her shoulders. 'You didn't have to do that. I'm a big girl. Anyway, I managed, and you were always at the other end of the phone when I needed to talk. You'd have been fed up with me by the end of the first day and champing to get away. I had to do it my way, and having you rant in my ear about my future when I couldn't hang up on you wouldn't have worked, for either of us.'

'You're probably right, but still...' He'd let her down. And himself. Again he wasn't sure why he thought that.

Raphael began pushing his friend's worldly goods towards the lift that'd take them to the car park. 'Bumped into Carly on Wednesday. She's pretty excited about you returning to the Queen Victoria.'

'She's more excited about her wedding. We've already got a night out planned with the other two from our training days' group. Funny how we're again all here at the same time. I wonder if that means everyone's settling down, becoming responsible adults, or is this just another stop along the way? Seems London's our place. My place?'

This sounded more like the Isabella he'd known for so long: always confident and putting it out there about how she wanted to live, and yet being gnawed at on the inside with her insecurities over people sticking by her, not breaking the bonds she desperately needed. Her parents had put her into boarding school when they felt she'd have better support and company than at home with them. They hadn't known a thing. He'd held her while she'd cried over being sent away. But after falling heavily for Cassie, and having her treat him so badly, he knew what a shattered heart felt like—and wasn't risking going there again. Nor hurting someone else similarly when he wasn't able to give enough of himself to her.

He said, 'Stop trying to second-guess everything, and enjoy being back amongst us all.' He would never desert her; he needed her friendship as much as she needed his. She understood him like no one else. If only he could stick with friendship, not let other emotions get in the way. 'You can do it. You have to believe in yourself.'

Then Isabella flicked him a look he couldn't interpret. 'Like you?' Her eyes were locked on his. 'I can follow your example? Work non-stop, get a home that I won't get to spend much time in?'

His happiness slipped. 'Is that what I've become? A workaholic?'

'It's what you told me only weeks ago.'

'I was probably trying to deflect you from your problems.' He'd been voicing his concerns about how everyone around him seemed to be finding love and making babies, while he was getting further tied up with work. What he hadn't said was how he wished he could find what it would take to try again, to finally put his past to rest. But he couldn't. Because of Cassie's selfishness, he'd lost a son and still wasn't able to make peace with himself about that.

'About those problems, will you always be here for me on the bad days?'

Where did that come from? *'Oui*, you can count on me.' She already knew it.

'Thanks. I can't tell you how good it is to spend time with you. It's been a while since anyone told me what to do.'

'Most people are too scared to.' He laughed. 'Let's get this load home and go have a drink and a pub meal to celebrate your arrival in London.' Better out somewhere surrounded by people than stuck in his kitchen together. Only now was he beginning to understand the coming weeks sharing his house might not be as comfortable as he'd thought. Which was so far left field it was crazy. Izzy would get busy beginning her new life, and he'd be hanging on to the dull but predictable one he'd made for himself.

'Sounds good to me. I loved the pub food when I lived here last time.' Isabella's hand tapped her stomach, then a hip. 'Not that it ever did me a lot of good. But I'm in for to-night anyway.' She threaded her arm through his, ignoring how the trolley aimed sideways and caused him to put more pressure on to controlling it with the other arm. 'Honestly, Rafe, I keep wanting to pinch myself. It's been for ever since we last saw each other. Talking on the phone or through the internet doesn't quite cut it. I like to know you're within reaching distance.' She gulped, tripped, righted herself and stared straight ahead. 'Talking too much. Put it down to jet lag, if that happens so soon after a flight.'

This was different. He hauled the brakes on the hope beginning to unfold deep inside. In the long run he wouldn't be enough for Izzy. She needed someone to love her unconditionally. That wouldn't be him after the way Cassie had blown his trust out of the water because Izzy had her own issues about believing anyone would love her enough to stay around. Anyway, give her a few days to settle in at work and catch up with the girls and she'd be off doing all sorts of random things, and then he could relax around her. 'You don't suffer from jet lag.' He'd always been envious when he'd had to grapple with debilitating exhaustion for days after a long-haul flight, while this woman usually bounced off the plane ready to party.

'Always a first time.' Isabella remained quiet until they reached his car. More unusual behaviour.

Something was up, and finding out what was imperative if he was to be onside as she settled into London for good, but best left alone today. He tipped his head sideways to stare at Isabella. Naturally he always wanted to help her when she was in difficulty, but normally he'd accept it if she refused to talk. But today he wanted to get behind the pain in the back of her eyes, see her achieve genuine happiness. Opening the car boot, he said, 'Let me do this. You get comfortable inside.'

'Like I'm your grandmother?' She smiled. 'How is Grand'mère, by the way? Fully recovered from her hip replacement?'

'Chasing the great grandkids with her crutch, apparently. Being her, she'll be back cycling around the city before she should,' he said with a smile. He adored Grand'mère. She was the only other person besides Izzy to support him in all his endeavours without criticism. His family loved him but always wanted to tell him what they believed he was doing wrong with his decisions. 'I was talking to her last night and she said whenever you need a change of scenery, pop over and spend time with her.' What she'd really said was, when Isabella was fed up with him, go pay her a visit and she'd sort her out. Grand'mère had a soft spot for the lost Kiwi girl who'd often hopped a train to go spend a day with her when she was working in Tours.

'Cool. I'll do that sooner than later. I love your grandmother, and Avignon's one of my favourite cities.' She handed him one of the smaller cases.

He shook his head. 'That big sucker first.'

'She might be just what I need on the days when you're not available for chewing your ear off.' Fixing a smile on her face she made to shift the bags. 'The family still as smothering as ever?'

Typical Izzy. Here he was holding back on the big questions and she just leapt in. 'Out of the way. This is man's work.'

'Whatever.' Her eye roll made him laugh.

At least she backed away from the stack of cases.

'What have you got in here?' he groaned. 'You must've paid a small fortune in excess baggage costs.'

'You avoiding my question?'

'You know I am. Now, get in the car before I put a bag on your seat and leave you to catch the train.'

Isabella snuggled into the soft leather seat and tugged her crumpled denim jacket across her chest to keep out the chill. From what she'd seen coming in to land, London had not turned on the sunshine in welcome, and the air out here was proving it. But Raphael had more than made up for the chilly welcome, hugging her tight as though he never wanted to let her go. There'd been relief in his gaze as she raced to him, as though he hadn't really believed she'd turn up.

Well, she was here, and right now she needed friends who didn't ask awkward questions. Count Raphael out, then. She sighed. He never let her get away with anything.

There again, he knew how to help her without seeming too intense. Demanding an instant decision about the job in the Queen Victoria had been unusual for him but just what she needed to get out of the blues she'd dumped herself into. Since his phone call determination to get on with consolidating her life had started growing, begun to fill the empty place deep inside, even excited her. There was a long way to go, but a start was way better than nothing at all.

The car rocked as Raphael clambered in beside her. 'Ready?'

She nodded. Fingers crossed, for everything. 'I sure am. What's Richmond like?' It was the suburb where he'd bought his house. 'I hear it's very pretty.'

'It is. There're plenty of fabulous cafés, and I enjoy walking or cycling along the river when I've had a rubbish day and need to put things into perspective.'

'That would be often.' He gave his all to patients. Studying him as he drove out of the airport, shock hit her.

He's changed.

His face was drawn, his movements heavier, his words spoken more thoughtfully. Why? Another sigh. He wouldn't thank her for asking so she changed the subject. 'How's Pierre?' His cousin's son held a special place in Raphael's heart.

'In love with the girl next door. Apparently he's going to die if she doesn't kiss him soon.' Raphael chuckled. 'Everything's so intense at his age.'

'Too much so sometimes.'

Rafe had been seventeen when he'd helped Adele during the birth of her son. He'd been driving her through the country lanes headed for the birthing centre when her well-spaced labour pains went out of control. He'd told Isabella there'd been no time for embarrassment with Adele gripping his arm and screaming to do something about the baby. The first birth he'd seen and aided, and from that day on he'd known what he wanted to do with his future career in medicine. 'Pierre's now a robust fifteen-year-old, and also thinking of going into medicine. Though not obstetrics. He's keen on cardiology, though that might have something to do with his heart being in torment at the moment.'

'You think?' Shuffling down further in her seat, Isabella stared out the window as they followed the main road leading into the city. 'This is familiar. I like familiar. It makes me feel I might be doing the right thing coming back.' She did feel connected to London, something she didn't get often. Wellington had been the only other place, and Darren's infidelity had altered that. Sure, he hadn't been the only one to get things wrong with their marriage, but he had broken her heart by seeking solace in other women's arms, and wrecked her trust in people.

'Papa and Maman have returned to live in the family home in Avignon. Dad's left the bank. It was getting too stressful so now he's working part time with a importing company and aiming to enjoy time out with the family.'

'That's huge.' Monsieur Dubois had worked long and hard most of his life. 'It's great news, isn't it?' Then her heart stuttered. Would Raphael move home now? Just when she'd returned to London? When she wanted to spend time with him?

Rafe was leaning forward, his concentration fixed on the road and cars ahead. His tight grip on the steering wheel was another giveaway he was rattled. *'Oui.'*

'But?' she dared to ask.

His fingers loosened their grip, tightened again. 'I'm still not ready,' he said in a 'don't go there' voice she knew not to ignore.

She closed her eyes and tipped her head back, let the silence take over. Better than saying anything to upset her friend. Apart from his parents almost suffocating him in love she had no idea what was behind his refusal to return home. He seemed more content than in those dark days after he and Cassie broke up, but there were times Isabella wondered how happy he really was with his lot.

The silence became uncomfortable. 'We had such plans growing up, didn't we? Nothing turned out anything like them.' There'd never been any doubt Raphael was going into medicine. He had intended setting up a private practice in his home city, while she'd thought she'd go into marketing, then car sales so she could drive to-die-for vehicles. Running a bar came into the plans somewhere around that time. But nothing had felt right, like something was missing as it was in her family. Then hearing Raphael talking about working with patients and the pain and fear and love that surrounded people when they were sick, she understood she wanted to work with people too. Not by handing them a full glass over a counter, but soothing their fears when they were injured, caring that they got through whatever was frightening them. So she applied to start training as a nurse, and had been the most at ease in her life for the next four years. Until she was qualified, and once again restlessness overtook her so finally, in desperation, she came to London and signed up for the midwifery course. Being there for those babies, and sharing—albeit on the periphery—the love and excitement every baby brought its parents, had made her happier than she'd ever believed possible. Having two options to her career was a bonus, and she had no intention of doing anything else career-wise. It was the one thing she was absolutely certain about.

'I am so glad you're here, Izzy.' Rafe sank back against the seat, and flicked her a quick smile, his knuckles no longer white and tight. Then he stiffened again. 'Not that I'll have a lot of free time to spend with you.'

It sounded like a warning of some sort. He wasn't available for friend time? Again, her heart stuttered. Which frightened her. *Raphael was a friend.* Couldn't be anything else. Of course they were never going to be anything else. These oddball jitters just went to show how far out of sync she'd become with what she needed from life. 'I'll be busy too,' she told him with a dollop of self-preservation for her pride. 'Finding a flat to rent, catching up with the girls, starting my new job.' A yawn caught her. Bed would be good right now. Damn but she needed some sleep, although past experience told her she was best to stay up till a reasonable hour, and eat a decent meal. Even then, there'd only be intermittent hours of unconsciousness. Glancing over to Rafe, for the first time in ages, pure happiness surged through her. It was as though she had come home, not left it. And she suspected she wasn't only thinking about London and friends, but Raphael in particular. Whatever that meant, she was too tired to worry about it. She let the silence return. Until again she couldn't stand it. 'I can't wait to see your house.'

He sucked in a breath. 'You're going to be disappointed. I'd be lying if I said it's a work in progress. I haven't done anything about the paintwork or getting the kitchen altered and the bathrooms modernised. I never seem able to find the enthusiasm or time.'

'Maybe I can help.'

His eyebrows rose in shock. 'I'm not talking a small job here.'

'Have to start somewhere, and if I'm going to get my own place eventually I might as well practise on yours first.'

'You think?' He grinned. 'Afraid I'm going to have to turn your offer—' he flicked a finger in the air '—down.'

'Coward.'

'Pink walls and floral curtains are so not my thing.'

'Mine either.' Her tastes were more along the lines of pale colours—more white than anything, lots of natural light, big empty spaces. That came from the real estate programs she'd watched avidly back in Wellington when she'd begun collecting furniture for the future house she and Darren were going to buy. 'Dark blue walls and carpets, a dash of white in the curtains, lime green furniture should do it.'

'Excellent. We have a plan.'

Isabella smiled. It was great how he said 'we.' As if she had a place in his life. But then she always had. Did that mean she'd be looking for a home in his neighbourhood? Doubt she could afford a dog kennel in Richmond. The idea of moving too far from Raphael suddenly irked, when it shouldn't. Friends moved around, came back together, moved on. At the moment they were in the coming back together phase. Who knew for how long?

'Here we are.' Raphael parked outside a brick row house. 'Welcome home.'

It wasn't her home, only a stop gap while she found somewhere for herself, but she'd take the warmth that went with his words and enjoy. Shoving the door wide, she clambered out on tired legs and looked around. Trees lined the street, a dog barked from behind a house next door and puddles glistened in the sun that was making its way out from behind the clouds. Home. Yes, it felt exactly like what she'd dreamed of having in Wellington. A house in a quiet neighbourhood. Throw in friends nearby, and Rafe had got it right when he chose this place. It was perfect.

Nothing's perfect. There're always faults.

The warning didn't dampen the warmth pushing aside her exhaustion.

Following Raphael inside, she stopped and stared at the hallway walls. Eek. 'Magenta? This is so dark it feels like it's falling in on us.' Definitely a fault.

'Wait until you see the kitchen.'

That colour had to go. Sooner than later. It was hideous. She shivered and traipsed behind Raphael up the stairs with the smallest of her cases in hand. It soon became obvious nothing had been done to spruce up the house for a long time, probably well before he moved in. Every room she peered into was in need of a coat of paint, preferably a very pale, neutral shade to lighten them, and new curtains to match. At the top of the stairs on the third floor he dumped the heaviest of her cases. 'This is your room for as long as you want it. It's the best of the two spares, and anyway I use the smallest for an office,' he told her before heading back down to get the next bag.

Isabella looked around the neat but bland room, and shrugged. No magenta in here, thank goodness, but the pale mauve reminded her of an old lady's room. Still, it was somewhere to put her head down, and give her time to find somewhere to rent. So why the flicker of excitement? Sinking onto the edge of the bed she rubbed her arms through her jacket, and said aloud to prove she wasn't dreaming it, 'I'm back in London, in the other country I call home.' Her mother came from the Lake District and she'd only visited her relatives once last time she lived here. The welcome mat had been in storage that day, something to do with her mother marrying a New Zealander instead of the lord of whatever they'd planned on having as a son-in-law, and Isabella being the offspring of someone less desirable, despite her father's mega career in the Foreign Service, hadn't changed their attitude. They should've got over it by now, but it seemed some things weren't meant to be, and she'd quietly headed away, deflated but resolute she wasn't going to beg for recognition.

'I'm glad. For both of us.'

Hadn't heard Raphael returning with another case, had she? Blinking, she looked up into the steady but shocked gaze coming her way. Why shocked? He hadn't expected to feel glad she was staying with him? No. He wouldn't have offered if he didn't want her here. Or would he these days? 'I made the right call. Thanks for letting me know about the job.' She couldn't wait to start. It would be a bonus working alongside Raphael. Another was the girls were also all working at the same hospital.

'*Aucun problème.* Now, there's a bathroom on the floor below. It's all yours as I've got an en suite bathroom attached to my bedroom. Help yourself to anything you want. The kitchen pantry's full and the freezer's holding some of your favourite fish.'

'A shower's what I need. And some clean clothes.' She sniffed her jacket and grimaced. 'Yuck. Long-haul travel has its own peculiar smell.'

He flinched, looked away. 'Take as long as you need. We're only going along the road for a drink and a bite to eat.'

Despite his reaction, that sounded so normal she laughed. This was what she'd come for. Normal. Whatever that was. At the moment everything felt right. Especially being with Raphael, knowing he'd never hurt her, no matter how far either of them pushed the boundaries of their friendship. Yes, packing up and coming here was a good move. Better than good; it was great, and filled with promise.

Believe it.

Yet she didn't feel quite normal with him. Yet. Still to come?

CHAPTER THREE

'HERE'S TO LONDON and your new job, and catching up with special friends.' Raphael held up his glass to tap Isabella's, just as loud laughter broke out further along the bar. 'Also to sorting out what's putting that sad look in your eyes whenever you think I'm not looking.'

Ignoring that last comment, Isabella tapped back. 'To spending time with you.' Except he'd already warned her he wouldn't be on tap all the time. They'd both opted to stick to soft drinks. She was wired. And exhausted. Even a little excited. Throw in worry about a whole heap of things she couldn't deal with right now, and she had the whole picture really. The trip in from the airport had touched her in an unexpected way. While it *had* felt like coming home, maybe being with Raphael was the reason. They understood each other so well, despite the awkward subjects they hadn't shared over the years. Cassie, the love of his life; and her truth about her marriage. She hadn't realised how much she'd missed his sharp remarks, though lately they seemed too sharp.

'Good luck with that. I struggle to find time to spend with myself.' His grin was lopsided and a little tight.

'Sounds like you need to find a life.' What was wrong? He wasn't known to forego having fun during his downtime, despite the serious side to the man who cared deeply for people worse off than himself.

'I bet you're about to sort me out,' he grumped. Then his grin became genuine. 'This could be a win-win for both of us. I could do with a kick up the backside.'

'Thanks for putting me up at short notice. I'll get on to other rental agencies ASAP.'

If I can't stay with you long term.

She choked. Stay with Raphael permanently? Where had that come from? So what was wrong with the idea? How about because they were friends? Sure, friends often shared accommodation, but she and Raphael had never lived in each other's pockets. Not even that time they'd worked together in Tours.

'No problem.' Raphael was suddenly intensely focused on the bar counter, his hands twirling his glass back and forth.

'I'll be out of your hair as soon as possible.'

I've only just got here, and I want to spend time with you. Need to, if I'm being honest, so that I can untangle the mess I've made of things by talking it out and then get on with living in London.

So she could get over this sensation of wanting more with him. Raphael usually kept her grounded. Today she was confused. Here was the reliable, helpful, caring Raphael she knew, and yet there was more. A deeper feeling that wanted to push hard at the walls, let him in in a new way. Into her heart. Her glass banged down on the counter. No. No way. She'd only let him down, and hurting him was not happening on her watch. Grabbing her glass again, she gulped down her drink.

Raphael had returned to watching her.

'Take your time. You've only just arrived.' His hand covered hers.

Whipping her hand away, she looked around the pub, frantically trying to still the wild thudding behind her ribs. 'Sure,' she muttered. This was not them. Glancing back at him, her heart did a funny little dance, while her eyes began tearing up. Rafe looked beyond stunning. He always had, yet she'd never really seen him as other women did. He was her friend. Nothing had changed. So why notice the stubble on his chin? Stubble was stubble, right? Or was it? Her palm itched. Reality check. Something had changed. Now she needed to focus on putting things back the way they used to be or move out of his house tomorrow. London Bridge was looking good.

'You cooked any French cuisine lately?' The question wasn't light-hearted. Was Rafe feeling her tension?

'Not really.' Darren had refused to eat anything he thought remotely French, all because of Raphael. So childish, but to keep the peace she'd thrown out the French recipe books and stuck with the boring basics: roasts, steak, sausages.

'We'll have to remedy that. Can't have you forgetting how to make a good béarnaise sauce.'

When she looked at Raphael she found a smile that held nothing back coming her way. Her stomach squeezed, while her heart filled with relief, returned to normal. See? Everything was fine. Time apart hadn't affected her perception of their friendship. It was the tiredness tripping her up, making her look at things differently. Today they were a little off centre, but that could be because she was now an ex-married woman he didn't know as well as he used to when she was single. 'Last time I saw you was in the bar further down this road. You'd put an offer in on a house and we were celebrating early because I wouldn't be around when the sale went through.' They'd also been toasting her moving back to New Zealand with her husband, though thinking back she remembered Raphael hadn't been too enthused about that. What she hadn't re-alised at the time: she was probably as much at fault as Darren. Which went to show she was utterly hopeless at relationships, not having had much experience other than snatching at friendships as and when they presented, because who knew how long she'd be staying around. Better keep that in mind if those odd feelings for Raphael returned.

'*Oui*.'

'You got drunk, and I had to get you home in a cab before you passed out.'

He winced. 'Sometimes your memory's too good.'

'What was that about anyway?' Rafe didn't do drunk, or drinking less than sensibly. Or very rarely and then only when something had gone horribly wrong for him.

'Can't remember.' He was looking everywhere but at her. 'Ah, here come the chips I ordered.'

Okay, the avoidance game. She should demand to know what he wasn't telling her, but she didn't want to spoil the rest of the evening. Past experience told her she'd eventually win, but she didn't have it in her tonight to do the hard grind to get there. Then she got a whiff of hot chips and relaxed. 'Yum. It's great to be catching up.'

That was the truth, no matter what else she might be feeling. Her legs were aching and her head filling with wool. But then she was starting over on the other side of the world to where she'd been two days ago, and for the first time ever, it was scary. Until now everything had been about making sure she had people with her, by her, there for her. After impulsively accepting the job at the Queen Victoria she'd then sat down and thought it through, and realised how tired of moving from one opportunity to the next she was. The Cambodian experience had shaken her, made her see how strong and enduring families could be for each other. It had made her understand she had to believe in herself before asking anyone else to. She couldn't keep winging it with any relationships. This move had to have a finality about it, *and* she'd go it alone so that eventually she might find herself equipped to give as much back as she needed for herself. More, in fact.

'Want another drink?' Rafe had the barman's attention. 'Izzy?'

Shaking away the questions filtering through the fog in her head, she pushed her drink aside. 'Can I have a water, please?' She studied Raphael for a moment. The gangly teen she'd first met had grown into a lean, muscular man with a face that said *Trust me*. A striking face that other women said made them think bed every time. Her stomach squeezed again, harder this time, showing how concerned she was becoming about him. Something wasn't adding up. Nothing to do with bed.

'You seeing anyone at the moment?' The question was out before she thought it through, but since when did she have to hesitate over asking him anything? He mightn't always be happy with her nosiness, or even give her an answer, but never had he made her uncomfortable over voicing what she wanted to find out. No idea why it felt so important to know where he was at with women, but it did, and she'd acted on those feelings. Being left in the dark was never an option. Knowing what was going on around her meant always being on top of problems before they erupted. Except when it came to her marriage. Then she'd been scared to face the truth, to accept she'd made a monumental mistake.

'*Moi?*' He tapped his chest, mock shock on his face. 'This is Raphael Dubois you are asking.'

'Yes, you, Rafe.' Good-looking men didn't hang around being single for ever, especially doctors in a hospital filled with females of all ages. He'd had his share of women. She knew because he'd talked about them sometimes. Never a derogatory word, always admiration, along with the old wariness about relationships and not trusting they'd last for ever.

His shock was replaced with genuine resignation. 'No. Nobody serious and usually nobody at all.'

She sat up straighter and reached for her glass, took a mouthful. Definitely something out of whack. She'd give him a break from the quiz. 'Tell me about my new job. Anyone I might know on the ward?'

'Not that I'm aware of. Your girlfriends

work in different areas, none on the maternity ward, but I guess you know that.'

'The emails have been flying back and forth. Carly's wedding is so close. Everyone's excited about that.' Now she had something genuine to grin about. 'Which reminds me. Do you want to come with me? The invitation is for Isabella and partner. You'll have to sit alone during the ceremony since I'm going to be a bridesmaid.' Once it was definite she'd be here for the wedding, Carly had insisted.

'No one else to invite?' He was smiling at her but there was a slight hitch in his voice.

'I want you to come. Otherwise I'll go on my own,' she added for good measure. Could be sounding pushy, because she didn't want to turn up at her friend's wedding without someone at her side. The other three girls were all loved up, and she'd only feel lonelier than ever. The odd one out. Unless Raphael was with her.

'Count me in, unless I'm on call that weekend. What's the date?' When she told him he scrolled through his diary. 'Free all weekend.'

'Great. You still happy with your position at the Queen Victoria?'

'Can't complain. It's turned out to be everything I wanted, and some.' He smiled. 'Perfect, really.'

What about Avignon? Returning there was always in the back of his mind. 'I'm glad. You deserve it.' Hopefully she'd be able to say the same about her new job. That would help steady her path to getting this move right.

'Same goes for you. You've just got to believe it.' His gaze was steady—and serious. He believed her, though maybe not fully *in* her. But then he did know her as well as she did herself.

'I will.'

'Say it again. This time with more determination.'

Heck, she'd missed that accent. Talking on the Net it didn't sound quite so deep and so French, more of a garbled mix. Oh, hell. This was weird. Rafe was a friend. 'I will,' she growled through her confusion.

'Isabella,' he growled back.

'So when I suddenly go into a tailspin and

make a beeline for the airport with my pass-port, you'll stop me and tell me to think about what I'm going to do?'

'It won't come to that.' He smiled at her, deep and true.

Suddenly she wanted to cry, and laugh. Coming over to join Raphael was *the* right thing to do. Which brought up more questions than answers. Thank goodness his phone rang then.

'Please be the ward,' Raphael muttered to himself as he tugged his phone out of his pocket. He needed to put space between Izzy's questions and himself. He'd gone from excited to see her to wary about spending too much time with her. Looking at the phone his heart sank. No reprieve coming.

'Hello, Cooper. How was the game?'

'Get your sorry butt up here now. Haley's in labour and you promised you'd be with us for the delivery.'

Okay, it was a reprieve. Haley was almost three weeks early, nothing to be concerned about. He stood and slipped his jacket on, the phone held between his ear and his shoulder. 'How far along is she?'

'The midwife said she's dilated four centimetres,' Cooper snapped. 'That was ten minutes ago.'

'Take it easy. There's a way to go yet,' Raphael told his friend. Fingers crossed the baby didn't suddenly decide to rush out. 'I'm on my way.'

Izzy stood up, drained her glass of water and slipped her bag over her shoulder.

Damn. Isabella.

'I'll come with you,' she said, solving his dilemma about taking her home and earning more wrath from his friend.

'Faster than fast,' Cooper growled, the stress growing every time he said anything. Fathers and their babies.

'See you shortly.' He nodded to the exit and followed Izzy outside. 'You could catch a taxi back to the house.' Give him some time away from those sad eyes. 'You're exhausted.'

'True, but it's still early and I always try to stay up until my normal bedtime when I've come off a long flight.'

He didn't have time to argue, and a minute later he was driving down the street away from the pub and heading to the Queen Victoria faster than fast. 'I met Cooper and Haley at the hospital. He's a general surgeon and she's a radiologist. This is their first baby,' he explained.

'Exciting.'

That wasn't how Cooper had sounded on the phone. Raphael pressed the accelerator harder, and concentrated on getting to the hospital as quickly as possible.

'Which birthing suite is Haley in?' he asked Claudia as he charged on to the ward.

'Four,' the midwife replied. 'She's reached six centimetres and stopped. Baby seems in two minds about coming out.' Then she glanced past him to Izzy, charging along with them.

'Claudia, meet Isabella Nicholson. She's starting here next week.'

'Hi, Claudia.' Isabella smiled. 'Great to meet you.'

'And you.' Claudia laughed. 'We are having the night from hell, more babies than beds.'

Raphael slowed before he entered the suite, turned to Isabella. 'You want to sit in the office for a while?'

She pulled up short. 'Of course.'

A bell sounded throughout the ward. Claudia muttered, 'I've got to see to that. I'll be back as quickly as possible.'

'There you are.' Cooper stood in the doorway. 'The contractions have slowed. Probably to give you time to get here.'

Raphael gripped his shoulder. 'There are a few speeding tickets coming my way you can pay for.'

'Who's this?'

'This is my friend I picked up from the airport this afternoon. Isabella, meet Cooper.'

As Cooper reached out to shake her hand, he asked, 'You're a nurse, aren't you?'

'Yes, and a midwife.' She never let that one go by.

'Come and meet Haley. She could do with a distraction.'

Isabella glanced at him. 'Okay?'

'Of course.' Raphael headed towards Haley, his teeth grinding. So much for putting distance between him and Isabella. 'Hi, Haley. I hear things have slowed down since Cooper phoned me.'

Haley grabbed his hand and burst into tears. 'I'm glad you're here. I thought I was going to have the baby without your help.'

'Not a lot I'll be doing other than monitoring the progress. You'll still be doing all the work.' He leaned down to kiss her cheeks just as a contraction tightened her body. His hand was in a vice. 'Breathe out slowly. That's it.'

'Easy for you to say,' Haley muttered as the tension let go. 'You're not the one going through hell here.'

'True. How far apart was that contraction from the previous one?'

'Five minutes,' Cooper answered for her.

'Five minutes, four, six. Who cares?' Haley began tensing again. 'Bet you haven't timed this one, huh? Standing around talking to your buddy like all is well in your world. Which it is. You're not the one going through this agony.'

Raphael struggled not to laugh. He'd heard it all before but to hear Haley talk so much was a surprise. 'And I thought you were shy.' She'd become a radiologist since they didn't have to talk to patients very often, mostly spent their days reading X-rays and MRIs.

'You can shut up too. Get on with making this baby come out.' Then she stared behind him. 'Who are you?'

Izzy stepped forward. 'Hello, Haley. I'm Isabella, Rafe's friend.'

'You made it, then. Raphael was unsure whether you'd turn up.'

I was? 'Hardly. When Isabella says she's going to do something, then there's no changing her mind.' She just didn't always last the distance.

Haley tilted her head at him. 'You've been on tenterhooks ever since she accepted the job here.'

'Lie still. I'm going to listen to baby.'

And shut you down before Isabella starts getting the wrong idea.

'Ah!' Haley cried. 'Here we go again.'

Cooper took her hand, held tight.

Raphael moved to the end of the bed, and gently lifted the sheet covering Haley.

'Are you comfortable lying down through the contractions?' Isabella asked when the current one was over.

'I prefer standing, but when one starts I can't get off the bed quick enough to see it through. I know I should sit on the side, ready to be hauled to my feet by Cooper. It's just that every way I sit or lie it's uncomfortable.'

'Want to try standing next time? I'll help you.' Isabella began rubbing Haley's back, easing out the knots that were no doubt in her muscles, and she started relaxing.

'All right.' Haley was surprisingly acquiescing.

Raphael made the most of Izzy's distraction to examine Haley. 'Eight centimetres. You're back in business.'

'Knew the little blighter was waiting for you to get here. Now there'll be no stopping him.' Cooper's tension had backed off some since he and Izzy had arrived.

Isabella was still rubbing Haley's back. 'Walking around the room might help too, could ease the pain some and get the labour moving along faster. What do you think?'

'I'll try anything. I just want this over.' Haley sat up and slowly slid her legs over the side of the bed. Then another contraction gripped her and Raphael and Cooper took an arm each and hauled her to her feet.

Cooper held her against him, whispering sweet nothings in her ear and rubbing up and down her sides. 'You can do this, darling.'

'Not a lot of choice,' she groaned through clenched teeth. She'd barely got through the contraction and another came. As it finished, she growled, 'Don't think I'll be walking anywhere at this rate.'

'Let's give it a go,' Izzy encouraged. 'Anything's worth a try.'

Raphael watched her with Haley. She had a way about her that made Haley relax. She was going to be an asset on the ward. And when the next contraction came she was right there, encouraging her while Cooper held his wife and murmured in her ear.

'I'm feeling pressure, like I need to push.

That's supposed to happen, isn't it?' Haley said some time later.

'Back on the bed,' Raphael told her. 'I'll take another look at what's going on.'

Izzy stood beside him. 'Looking good.'

'It sure is.' Raphael grinned. 'Baby's crowned. Let's get him out here so we can all met the little man.'

Cooper took Haley's hand. 'Come on, darling, give it everything you've got.'

'What do you think I've been doing?' This time there was no anger, only exhaustion, in her voice, and she gave her husband a smile before drawing in a breath and beginning to push.

Raphael glanced across to Izzy, who was back to rubbing Haley's tense back muscles. 'That's it. You're doing great.' She looked up at him and smiled as though to say, 'I love this job.'

He grinned. So did he. Bringing babies into the world had to be the best experience he could have. And when the baby was his friends' he couldn't be happier. 'And again,' he told Haley. 'The shoulders are out.' Then,

'One more push.' Moments later he held a tiny, new human being in his large hands, quickly checking him over before gently laying the baby on Haley's stomach. 'Haley, Cooper, meet your son.' Blink, blink. Damn it, he wasn't supposed to get emotional over this, but these two deserved this moment. 'Izzy, Cooper wants to cut the cord. Could you assist, please?'

'Sure.' She found gloves on the trolley to pull on and helped Cooper cut the cord when it had stopped pulsing.

Raphael watched as Izzy carefully wiped the baby with a towel. She looked so right doing that. What would she be like with her own baby? Besotted, no doubt. But like all midwives she'd probably be a nervous wreck over doing something wrong when she knew exactly how to look after a newborn. Now she carefully lifted the baby and wrapped him in a clean towel before handing him back to his mother, a look of awe on her tired face.

Raphael tapped her on the shoulder, nodded towards the door. 'We'll give you time to bond. Just holler if you want anything.'

For once Cooper was silent, and Haley seemed to have returned to her normal quiet self.

Outside the suite, Izzy leaned against the wall, and grinned. 'Wow. It never changes, does it? The thrill that comes with a baby arriving in our hands?'

'It certainly doesn't.' Not caring who saw him, he pulled her into a hug. 'Welcome home, Izzy.'

Her body tensed. Then relaxed. 'Yes, at last.'

Late the next morning Raphael nudged the shower off and reached for his towel. The tension in his legs put there by a harder than usual run had at last diminished under the onslaught of hot water. Outrunning the images of Izzy rushing at him in the arrival terminal, her wide-eyed gaze as she explored his house and yawning into her chips at the pub hadn't worked. Then there was the one after where they'd returned from the hospital and he'd helped her up the stairs to the third floor and the bedroom that was temporarily hers, her body struggling to put one foot in front of the other as exhaustion outdid everything else. He'd nearly swung her up into his arms to carry her up there, but common sense had stepped in just in the nick of time, forcing him to take her arm instead. Once he'd not have hesitated, but now the very thought of getting close to her and then letting her down was frightening.

After pulling on knee-length shorts and an open-necked shirt he tidied up his room, and made the bed. Earlier, when he'd popped into the kitchen to grab his keys on the way out for his run, he'd been saddened by the empty water bottles on the bench, evidence that Isabella had been downstairs during the night. The way she'd been all but comatose when they'd got home she should've slept right through the night without once opening her eyes. Something needed doing pronto about her insomnia. That sort of tiredness undermined everything a person did if left too long.

He hadn't reckoned on being quite so rattled on seeing her yesterday, and hearing her laugh and talk. Except it'd been Izzy with a difference. The laughter was strained, the conversations awkward. His heart had stirred at the sight of her, which once he'd have said was because of their friendship, yet now felt it might be about something more intense. They loved each other, platonically. But no denying that since the day he'd had to watch her marry Darren he'd felt he'd lost something, that he loved her in a way he shouldn't. Not that he trusted his feelings. Look where love had got him last time. He'd fallen fast and hard, and gave Cassie everything, only to have her continually complaining it wasn't enough. And that was before her final treachery.

When Isabella first told him she and Darren were splitting his heart had soared with selfish relief. Then, as the sordid details of their marriage registered, he'd been angry and distressed for her. Since then his emotions had run the gamut from hope to despair and everything in between for her. And for himself. Something he only admitted at four in the morning when sleep was elusive.

Now he had to cope with Izzy living in his own space, however temporarily. A space she'd slotted into last night as easily as he'd seen her shrug into a puffer jacket in midwinter on the Rhône years ago. Nothing unusual in that. Except he also had to ignore how his heart was involved. Cassie had finally taken a back seat. But not the loss of his child. He'd never forgive her for that, which meant his heart wasn't ready for anyone else.

Goosebumps lifted on his forearms. Rubbing hard did nothing to knock them down. Nor did the light woollen jersey he pulled over his head in the bedroom. His nose twitched. Coffee vapour was filtering up the stairs. Coffee. Had to be the answer. Obviously Izzy was in the kitchen. Damn, no dashing into the hospital for a bit of time out.

She was leaning one hip against the bench, a full mug wrapped in her hands, and a bewildered smile lifting her lips as she glanced down at the creature rubbing against her legs. 'You've got a cat.'

'I rescued her from the RSPCA.'

'Yeah, but you and a pet?'

'Since I was a little guy I've wanted a dog.

Now that I'm settled it was time to do something about it.'

Isabella blinked, then laughed. 'Do I need to point out this is a cat?'

'Her name's Chienne.'

'Dog? You are so mean.' She put her mug aside and picked up the cat to snuggle against her breast. Ah, chest. Nope, definitely breasts, the rounded shape filling her T-shirt perfectly.

'That's me,' he muttered, and reached for a mug.

She rubbed her chin on Chienne's head. 'What was your real name before this mean guy got hold of you?'

'According to the RSPCA, Waster was on the tag around her collar. I was not going to keep calling her that.'

'So you came up with something even more original.' Izzy blinked and looked down at her furry bundle. 'I bet you're spoilt rotten. Raphael has never been mean.'

A band of warmth wrapped around him. It felt good to hear that, and while nothing was wrong in his life, who couldn't do with the odd compliment or two? 'Cover her ears while

I say that I'd prefer a dog but they need so much attention and given my erratic and long hours it wouldn't have been fair to get one.'

Izzy began nibbling her bottom lip, which was new to him.

'What's up? You look like you're not sure where you are.'

She blinked and reached for her mug to sip the steaming liquid. 'I know exactly where I am, yet I feel kind of lost. Could be my brain hasn't kept up with the rest of me and will be arriving later.'

'Or it might be because this is the final move of your life.' That'd be confronting for her. If she meant it. Except she'd tried that once before and look where that got her. Back here. Though not alone. *I'm here.* 'I remember feeling a little bewildered the day I moved in here and dumped my few possessions on the table I'd ordered from the local furniture store, along with a lounge suite and a bed.' The second bed in the room Isabella was using had arrived on Friday after a frantic phone call to organise that and a chest of drawers for her. 'I struggled to believe this was *my* home.' He tapped his chest with his knuckles. 'And that I got to stay here until *I* decided otherwise.'

'It's real, isn't it?' Isabella seemed to be holding her breath.

Expecting the right answer from him?

Sorry, Izzy, but I only know what's right for me, and I'm not sure I've got that right yet.

'It's as real as you want it to be.'

Her mouth quirked. 'Back at me, huh?' Then she hit the serious button. 'No regrets?'

'Honestly? No. Sometimes I think about how my life might have turned out if I'd let Cassie talk me into moving to Paris, but...' He shrugged.

Izzy's eyes widened at the mention of his ex, but she just stroked the cat.

Raphael filled his mug with coffee before topping up hers. Time to get on to something normal and ordinary. 'I'm going in to see Haley and baby as soon as I've had this. Want to come?' Gulp. That was not what he planned on saying.

'Give me ten to take a shower, and fix up the face.'

It was going to take a fair amount of make-up to hide the shadows under her eyes, but he wasn't saying. 'There's no hurry.' Tell that to his taut body. He wanted to be doing something other than standing in his kitchen drinking coffee and smelling Izzy's perfume instead of the coffee. But he'd have to be patient.

Oui.

'I'll introduce you to whoever's about. You can also meet the three little guys I told you about a couple of weeks ago. They're something else. Their mum wants a quick word with me too.'

She paused on her way out of the kitchen. 'They've got to you, haven't they?'

'Just a little.' He'd love to have a family of his own. There'd be no replacing the son he lost but could it be time to think about moving on?

No. He wouldn't survive that sort of pain again.

CHAPTER FOUR

'HELLO, HALEY,' ISABELLA said to the happy woman cuddling her son in the single room where she'd been transferred after the birth. 'How're you feeling today?'

'Isn't Ryan the cutest baby ever?' Haley's eyes lit up. 'I can't believe I'm a mother.'

She'd soon get used to that with sleepless nights and nappies to deal with. 'Believe me, you are. I saw it happen.'

'So did I.' Raphael laughed from the other side of the bed. 'Can I have a hold?' He held out his arms.

Haley reluctantly handed him over. 'One minute.'

'Then it's my turn,' Isabella said. 'How are you doing with breastfeeding?'

'Eek. That's no fun. I can't quite manage it yet, but I've been told that's normal.'

'Certainly is. You'll soon get the hang of it. Don't stress though. That only makes matters worse.' She looked at Raphael. There was a look of relief in his expression. As though he didn't quite believe the outcome of Haley's labour would be so good. Which didn't add up considering there were no complications. Or was he thinking about children, as in his own? Why not? Could be his biological clock was ticking? That wouldn't be just a woman's prerogative. Deep in her tummy she felt a twinge, as though her clock had come to life. Her mouth dried. That was not part of the plan to settle here. Not yet, not until she'd got all the other factors right. In the meantime she'd get her fix holding other people's babies. 'Time's up.' She held out her arms for Ryan, and laughed at Rafe's reluctance to hand him over.

Haley was watching her son, hunger in her eyes, and Isabella couldn't not pass Ryan back to his mum. 'There you go. I'll have another turn before we leave.'

'Come and meet the triplets,' Rafe said as they left the room.

The moment they walked into the nursery Isabella felt the same awe she'd seen in Raphael's face when he talked about the three little boys. They lay in their cribs lined up side by side, blinking at any movement made by the two people leaning over them, smiling and chatting as though the boys understood. Raphael went straight across and gazed down at the babies too, warmth in his eyes. But also a shadow of something else. Anger? Pain?

'Hello, Raphael.' The mum turned to him. 'You didn't have to come in on your day off.' Her gaze shifted to Isabella. 'I know you don't get a lot of time to yourself as it is. Your partner must get fed up with you being called out all the time.'

He blinked and those emotions were gone. He was back to professional doctor mode. 'Melody, it's fine. I was coming to see another patient anyway. And this is Isabella Nicholson. She's a nurse and midwife, and will be starting on this ward later in the week.' Not his partner. Though he hadn't actually put it into words, it was there. Raphael nodded at the man gazing down at the boys with a besotted look. 'Isabella, this is Ollie, the doting dad.'

'Hello, Melody, Ollie. Your boys are gorgeous.' Isabella smiled. 'Look at them. They're so busy, moving their arms and kicking their little legs. You're going to have your hands full when you get them home.' Even the smallest boy, still attached to more monitors than his brothers, was staring up at everyone.

'Aren't we? And I can't wait.' Ollie grinned. 'Antony's taking a little longer to get up to speed, but really, we've been so lucky. These other two are already putting on weight. The sooner we're all at home, the better.'

'I don't want to rush things,' Melody said with a worried glance at Raphael. 'What if I can't cope?' She looked to Isabella. 'I've never had much to do with babies before. To have three at once is daunting. Not that I don't want them,' she added hastily. 'We've waited too long for this as it is.'

Ollie brushed a kiss across his wife's forehead. 'You'll be fine, sweetheart. With the folks dropping in to help and the daily visits from the district nurse, we'll manage.' He grinned. 'You'll soon be telling everyone to get out of the way and let you get on with looking after your boys.'

Raphael nodded. 'You'll be more tired than you've ever been, and there won't be enough hours in the day, but you'll manage. I promise. Even mothers with one baby for the first time go through the same concerns that you have. If you'd taken them home within a couple of days of them being born as usually happens when it's only one baby, you wouldn't have had time to think about all the things that need doing—you'd be doing them.'

'So everyone keeps telling me.' Melody sighed. 'But what if I'm useless as a mother?'

'Stop it,' Ollie growled softly. 'We're going to be the best parents ever. We're doing this together, remember?' He turned to Isabella. 'I've turned our back bedroom into an office so I can work from home for the foreseeable future. Whenever clients need to see me I can meet them there or at the company rooms in town.'

The worry in Melody's eyes only increased,

as though nothing was registering except she had three babies to look after and all the things that could go wrong. Was she a candidate for postnatal depression? Isabella glanced at Raphael, and relaxed. He was on to it. Of course the same thought would've occurred to him.

He said, 'I'll arrange for you to talk to someone about how you're going to cope, Melody. Try not to get too wound up about everything. Make the most of this time in here where you can learn a lot about being a mum in preparation for going home. Enjoy your babies. They grow up so darned fast you'll soon be wondering where the time went.'

Ollie lifted one boy—Shaun, according to the card on his little cot—and held him out to his mother. 'Here you go, Mum.'

Melody immediately relaxed and placed her son against her breast, rubbing his back as though she'd always been doing that.

'See, just like a pro.' Isabella nodded. 'He's as happy as can be, snuggling against you.'

'He's hungry.' The father picked up Antony and held him in a similar position.

'Aren't they always?' she said, and leaned over the third crib. 'Hello, Morgan. Aren't you the cutest little guy?' He was blinking and moving one hand in the air. So innocent and trusting. What would his life be like? All their lives? Would the three of them watch out for each other? Or compete over everything? If she'd had a sibling she was certain her life of moving from country to country would've been different. There'd have been someone who was always there, a constant, someone of a similar age to understand what she'd longed for, to share the good and bad times, to love always. Not all siblings got along though. There was that. No point thinking about what couldn't be changed. She was grown up now, and making her own way without having to do as her parents demanded. Besides, she'd had Raphael in her life since she was a teen. Still did. As good as a brother. *Brother?* These feelings she was getting for him had nothing to do with a brother.

Behind her, he was talking to Melody. 'I hear you've got another infection in your Caesarean wound.'

'Yes, but why when I've been taking antibiotics? It's not fair.' Melody sounded close to tears.

'We'll try a different antibiotic. Mind if I have a look first?'

Melody shook her head.

'Isabella, do you want to get me some swabs?' Raphael asked when he saw Melody's inflamed wound. 'They're in the trolley outside the door.'

'Sure.' She pushed the trolley into the room and slipped gloves on before handing him the swabs. 'You want the antiseptic fluid?'

'Please.' He cleaned the area and dabbed the yellow liquid all over. 'There, that should help. I'll make sure someone does that regularly. And I'll sign a prescription for the nurses to collect. Any other worries?' When Melody shook her head, Raphael said to Isabella, 'I'll go check on my other patients. You okay finding your way around?'

'You can introduce me to whoever's at the station and I'll go from there.' Though right now she'd be happy lying down for a nap. 'If you can't find me I'll be curled up somewhere out of the way.'

Raphael was quick to look at her, worry now in *his* eyes. 'Are you all right? This is so not like you.'

'The jet lag's new, I admit. But I haven't been sleeping well for so long I hardly notice.' Ever since she'd been forced to face up to the fact she hadn't married Darren purely for love but mostly for the security and one-stop life he'd promised. That had been as important to her as love. Maybe even more. It had taken her reaction to finding her husband in bed with another woman to bring her up sharp, and to start thinking about why she'd married in the first place. She hadn't liked the answers. They had her questioning her ability to have a loving, caring relationship. She'd been selfish in wanting the lifestyle Darren offered before anything else. Didn't mean he had to betray her though. How was she supposed to trust any man with her heart again?

'We'll talk some more about this when we're back home.'

'Ah, no, we won't.' She wasn't ready for

that. It was history, and she was getting on with *now*. 'Come on, play nice and introduce me to whoever's here.'

Two nurses were sitting in front of computers in the work area, and looked up at the same time. 'We were wondering if you'd drop in, Raphael. Mrs Baxter has been seen by the duty specialist and has settled down again.'

'No one let me know that.' He didn't look happy. 'But since I'm here I'll talk to her.'

One of the nurses was on her feet instantly. 'I'll come with you.'

'First let me introduce Isabella Nicholson to you.'

The same nurse turned to her. 'You're starting here later this week, aren't you? I saw your name on the roster. Hi, I'm Annabel, and this is Mary. What are you doing in here today? Should be making the most of your days off.' Annabel's eyes flicked from her to Raphael, a question in her gaze.

'Hello. I came along for the ride.' Not going to explain why she was with the handsome doctor who obviously had one of the nurses in a bit of a lather. Which was odd, because she was usually quick to let women know she was his friend, not his lover.

'Can you show Izzy around, Mary?' Izzy, not Isabella. Rubbing it in how friendly he was with her?

'Sure.' The other nurse stood up. 'Anything would be better than doing the stock figures.' Then she grimaced. 'Sorry, Isabella. That sounded all wrong. Take no notice of me.'

Isabella laughed. 'Don't worry. I'll get over it.'

'Want a coffee first?'

It might help her stay awake. 'That'd be great.'

'Come through to the staff kitchen, then. The lockers are along here too, and uniforms are next door.'

'It's all coming back.' When Mary shot her a puzzled look she explained, 'I trained as a midwife in this hospital, and spent many nights on this ward.'

'In that case, shall we grab coffees and go back to the station so I can keep an eye on things while interrogating you?' It was said with a smile, and Isabella laughed.

'Not sure I've got anything interesting to say, but let's give it a go.' As long as she didn't want information on Rafe. That would not be happening. His details were not for her to share.

'Actually, I did hear you'd worked here before. It slipped my addled brain. Esther and I are friends.'

'How is she? I only got here yesterday so haven't had a chance to catch up with her or our other two friends. The four of us trained together, and now we're all back here again.'

'She's great. Totally in love with Harry with stars in her eyes all the time.'

'Isn't it awesome?'

Mary handed her a mug and pushed the coffee jar in her direction. 'Help yourself.' Leaning back against the bench she watched Isabella. 'You're close to Raphael? Since he brought you in I figured you must've been together when he got the call,' she added hurriedly when Isabella tightened her mouth.

'We're friends from way back.' That wasn't divulging anything that could be twisted into something more interesting. 'It's been a while since we had time together.'

And that's all I'm saying.

'Lots to catch up on, then.'

Time to change the subject. 'So do you do all shifts or weekends only?'

'I cover all the rosters just like you're going to do. Most of the staff do, apart from two nurses who work nights only, and one who only does weekends. Where were you last working?'

'Based in Wellington, New Zealand, but I volunteered in Cambodia recently.' When they were seated in the workstation sipping coffee, Isabella filled her in on her working background and avoided questions about her private life. She was here, that's all that mattered. In fact, that was a good line to follow herself. 'What's the social life like here? Does everyone get together for drinks at the end of the week?'

'Some of us do. You up for that?'

'Absolutely. It's the best way to get to know people.'

Her eyes were heavy, and her head thick

with sleep. She shook herself and straightened up in the chair. Where was Raphael? He seemed to be taking a long time.

A phone rang and Mary reached for it, then brought up the computer screen. 'Here we go. Knew the quiet spell was too good to be true.'

Isabella looked around the work area, saw nothing unusual to ask about. All fairly standard. It wasn't going to be hard to slot in with everyone. A yawn slipped out and her eyes drooped.

'Wake up, sleepy head.' A firm hand shook her gently.

Isabella dragged her chin up off her sternum and blinked up at Raphael. 'Guess I didn't make the coffee strong enough.'

'Let's get out of here. You're giving everyone the wrong impression.' He winked.

All very well to make a joke of it, but she probably was. There seemed to be more people wandering around the area now. Saturday afternoon brought friends and family out in their droves. 'I'll be fine by the time I start work on Wednesday.'

Mary laughed. 'Seems I bored you to sleep

talking about shifts and who's who on the roster.'

Didn't hear any of that. 'Sorry. I'll do better next time. I'm still getting over my flights.' She stood up slowly, picked up her bag from the floor where it had fallen. 'See you when we're on the same shift.'

Mary nodded. 'Or handing over.'

'Do people know I'm staying with you?' Isabella asked Raphael as they waited for the lift to take them down to the car park.

'I haven't mentioned it to anyone except Jacki, since she's the head nurse for the ward, and I figured she needed to know since I put such a good word in for you.' He grinned. 'It's none of anyone else's business though. Not that it's a secret, but I don't want someone saying I'm favouring you once you're working amongst us.' The lift rattled to a stop and the door cranked open. 'Come on, let's get out of here and go do something interesting.'

'Like what?'

'For you that means getting some sleep.'

'If I sleep during the day I won't get much during the night.'

'The problem with that theory is that you're already dropping off every opportunity you get. And you don't sleep at night anyway.'

Isabella grimaced. 'True. How about I have a snooze, then we go for a walk along the river?' The exercise would do her good.

They climbed into Raphael's car and started for home.

'Want to talk about why you're so tired?' he asked quietly as they waited at traffic lights.

'Not really.' It wouldn't change things. But this was the one person she used to tell everything.

'Don't blame the jet lag. This is worse than normal.'

'Didn't mention the jet lag.'

'It's to do with Darren, right?'

Just spill the beans, get it off your chest. What's Raphael going to say that you haven't already said to yourself?

'I stuffed up big-time.' She paused, stared out the window at the tail lights on the car in front. 'I'm talking about my marriage. Our bust-up wasn't all Darren's fault.'

'There're usually two sides to these things.'

Yeah, but she was uncomfortable with her contribution, or lack of. 'I didn't love him as much as I should've.'

'Then why did you marry him?' There was genuine confusion radiating from Raphael. Maybe a hint of disappointment.

Shouldn't have told him. But she'd started, so might as well get it over. 'Because I thought I did. I *believed* I did. Right up until it all began disintegrating.'

No, earlier than that. I stayed in denial for as long as I could.

'The pain wasn't as deep as you'd expect?' Forget disappointment. Raphael was looking confused. Which made no sense at all. More to think about when she wasn't so tired.

'Yes, it was, but for the wrong reasons. That took a bit to figure out but when I did it hurt more than ever.' She drew a deep breath and rushed on. 'Darren promised a home and family, and to live in the same city for the rest of our lives. I so desperately wanted that I didn't look beyond to anything else. By marrying him I let him down. Hell, I let myself down. And you know what's the worst? I don't know with complete certainty that I've learnt my lesson. What if I make the same mistake again? I was so intent on living the life my parents had denied me I got it all wrong, and it worries me.' What if she fell in love again, only to find she'd made another mistake?

They'd stopped at another set of lights and Raphael's fingers were playing a silent tune on the steering wheel. 'We all make mistakes, Izzy.'

'I got wrong the one dream I've had most of my life.' She swallowed a bitter mouthful of pain. 'Which is why in the meantime I'm sticking to running solo and making a home of my own, by me for me. I don't want to hurt someone else. Better to play safe.' Get it, Rafe? Actually, it was her she needed to remind of that.

'I think you're being hard on yourself.'

'Yeah, right,' she growled. 'Easy for you to say. Darren did some bad things like those affairs and spending more time with his mates than me, but if I'd loved him as much as I'd professed, then he wouldn't have had to. He might've stayed home more often, might've been happy to go house hunting instead of skirt chasing.' She was grasping at straws. According to the partner of one of his mates, Darren had always had a roving eye. Not that it was his eye doing most of the work. But apparently she wasn't the only partner he'd cheated on, just the first wife.

'He could've talked to you about it, not buried his head in the sand.'

'Like Cassie did with you?' Isabella snapped, and instantly regretted her words. This was about her and her messed-up relationship, had nothing to do with Raphael's history. But he didn't seem to accept she was at least trying to take some of the blame in an attempt to soften the hurt Darren had created and that riled her. As he said, she was usually so honest it could be awkward. 'I shouldn't have said that.'

'*Non.* You shouldn't have.'

Silence took over in the car, tense and uncomfortable. Isabella stared out at the passing buildings, not really noticing them, instead seeing Wellington on a bright summer's day with the harbour sparkling and the ferries passing further out. Her heart didn't flutter with longing, instead seemed to sigh with relief. Yes, she'd done the right thing in leaving there, as she had in walking away from her marriage. And from now on she was dropping the worry about that, looking forward, no more doubts. Hopefully then the trust issue would start to resolve itself, and she could consider a new relationship. She'd make herself get on with it. Now. Not tomorrow or next week. Now. 'So what did you have in mind for us to do this afternoon?'

Raphael drew in a lungful of air and sighed it back out. He could hear Izzy's distress, understand her fear of repeating her mistake—because he knew it all too well himself. Cassie had torn his heart to shreds, and he was reluctant to try again. Hell, in the beginning he'd given Cassie *everything*. His love, his life, his family, trust. He'd only put his foot down about living in Paris because he already had the job he needed to set up his career as he wanted. It had been the only thing he'd denied her, and it had backfired, brought out her fickleness. So no, he wasn't getting involved with anyone else. Certainly not the woman sitting beside him. Then he went and messed with that idea. 'Thought we'd get the bikes out and go for a spin alongside the river.'

'We what?' Shock filled her face. 'Me? On a bike? Think you've got the wrong person in mind for that.'

He'd made her forget what she'd been gnawing her lip over though, hadn't he? Her lip was swollen. A kiss might help ease the soreness. Swearing under his breath, he scrabbled around for something inane to say. 'One of the doctors was selling her bike last week so I bought it for you.'

'Hope you got crash pads and a helmet and padded clothing to go with it. And a pair of those thick fancy shorts that make butts look bigger.'

Butts. Bigger. Fitted shorts. He swallowed hard. Sure. 'You forgot the steel-capped boots.' Even to his ears, his laugh sounded strained. But he was glad to have made her smile, though he was still sour about her snide remark over Cassie, even if it was true. That was just Isabella putting up the wall to keep him away. Though she had gone for the jugular, not something she usually did.

He'd never told her the whole story. Certainly hadn't mentioned the baby he'd only learned about when he'd tracked Cassie down a couple of years later. Nearly as bad was coming to terms with the fact Cassie should've been more upset, but relieved their baby hadn't suffered. Her new career in acting had been taking off and a baby would've been a hindrance. Later he learned the bit parts hadn't flowed into roles of any significance, had instead ebbed away to the point she now worked in a sleazy bar on the outskirts of Los Angeles, struggling to make ends meet. It was the last time he'd seen her, and he'd woken up. They had nothing in common, and he'd wondered how he could've loved her so much. They said love was blind, and he'd found out the hard way how true that could be. He didn't want to lose his sight ever again.

'Honestly, Rafe, I haven't ridden a bike since I was a teenager.'

'Which means your backside and legs will ache afterwards.' The way Izzy's backside filled out her shorts and trousers set his body aflame. 'No, you're right. Better I go alone and get home earlier.'

'You're backing out now?' She turned to face him.

There was no winning with Izzy. 'Let's stop somewhere for a late lunch instead.'

'Your shout for winding me up.' Her mouth spread into a cheeky smile and they were back on track, tension about their pasts forgiven.

But not forgotten. One day he'd find the courage to tell her the rest of the Cassie story. But not today. He'd hate to see pity in her eyes. 'Wouldn't have it any other way, *mon amie*.' Except friends didn't make his gut tighten over a smile. This was getting out of hand. He needed breathing space, which would be hard to find while they shared his house and worked on the same ward.

'How about we have a French week?' She'd

know exactly what he meant. It wasn't the first time, and probably wouldn't be the last. 'Everywhere we go except at the hospital.' Probably get locked up for speaking nothing but French there.

'Je ne veau pas faire de vélo.'

'Dure.'

Too late he realised how intimate spending time talking in his native language might be. He grimaced, then went with cheeky. 'I don't need to teach you to ride. Your body will remember how to push the pedals even if you cry foul, so toughen up.'

'Does this mean you're cooking dinner tonight? I'd like coq au vin.'

'Say that in French and I might oblige,' he replied in French. Actually, she wasn't too rusty, but he'd keep at her as it'd been a while since she'd been submerged in the language and he intended taking her back to Avignon to visit Grand'mère in the next few weeks.

And that idea had nothing to do with the feelings he wasn't admitting even to himself.

Or did it?

CHAPTER FIVE

RAPHAEL SLIPPED INTO the seat opposite Isabella in the hospital cafeteria with a mug of coffee in one hand and a large egg mayo sandwich in the other. 'What are you doing here?'

'Initiation course.' At eight that morning Isabella had received a call from the head nurse of the maternity ward to come in and do the drill all newly signed-on employees had to partake in.

'Damn, sorry, I was meant to tell you about that.'

'Apparently.' Forcing a laugh, she tried not to notice how Raphael's shoulders shaped his suit to perfection. That *perfect* word again. It popped up a lot around Rafe. But how his body filled his clothes? This was Raphael. Seems when she got jet lag she got it bad. 'No problem. It's the same old, same old. Work in one large hospital and you know the routine for any others you go to.' She'd spent the last few hours learning the ropes of where fire extinguishers and staircases were, as well as all the safety rules involving staff. 'Lunch is the best bit so far, even if beyond late.' It was nearly two and she was starving.

He blinked. 'Not same old food, then?'

'Nothing different about that, but it's far more interesting being in here.' Her hand swept the room. 'There are real people in here, not sheep following Miss This-Way-Folks all over the hospital.'

Raphael's laugh sent ripples of warmth through her. He was watching her closely. Looking for what? 'You seem a lot more awake than I've seen since you arrived. The jet lag must be wearing off,' he said.

'How was surgery?' He'd left home before six as his surgical list had four ops, one of which he thought might throw up some complications, and he'd wanted to be prepared. Nothing unusual there.

Now he nodded once, a grim expression

on his face as he glanced around them. 'The woman I told you about? The cancer has gone through to the uterus, as I'd suspected. Then when we had that sorted she haemorrhaged from the large bowel and we found another growth. I had to call in David Stokes, one of the general surgeons, to take over when I'd done all I could.' He shook his head. 'Some people get a raw deal.'

It wasn't sounding good for the woman. 'Take it easy. You've done all you can.' Isabella reached for his hand, squeezed it before letting go in a hurry. That wasn't a normal gesture from her to Raphael. But he was so distressed she could almost see anguish oozing out of his pores. It was also there in the tightness of his shoulders and the white lines around his mouth.

'I know. It's up to the oncologists now. She's only forty-one.' His frustrated sigh cut through her, had her wanting to take his pain for him.

One reason for preferring midwifery to nursing patients that specialists like Raphael dealt with was not having to face some of these grim cases. 'If you're not too late finishing tonight do you want to go out for a meal?' In her lap her fingers crossed of their own accord. Knowing doctors had little control over their private hours she didn't really expect an instant acceptance.

'Sounds like a plan.' Where was the enthusiasm?

'Look, we can give it a miss if you'd prefer.'

He looked straight at her. 'If I knock off about six will you hang around in town? I'm thinking we can go along the river to this bar everyone frequents. You'll like it.'

'That's a yes, then.' Raphael hadn't said no, or maybe; he'd said he'd be there. Yippee. Suddenly the ho-hum day had become bright and exciting.

Careful. This is your friend. He won't see it as a hot date.

Nor should she. Yeah, but it was growing on her that she'd come home, as in found her niche. Being with Raphael relaxed her in ways she hadn't known for a long time—for two years, really. Was that what close friends did? Or was there another reason for this deep sense of belonging whenever she was with him? If only she could sort out her mixed-up feelings for him. Slowing her breathing, she went for calm. 'Great, I'll be around here somewhere. Might see if Carly wants to go for a coffee and catch up while I wait for you. She's on days this week.'

'I need to tell you—you'll probably get a call asking if you mind starting on the ward tomorrow instead of Wednesday. We're three staff down and as busy as can be,' Raphael told her. 'Don't feel pressured to say yes. I know you're still tired and taking naps like a toddler.' His smile sent ripples throughout her body, which was frankly weird. He shouldn't make her feel like this. Except apparently he did.

'I'll be fine, might even be better for doing something. If not, there's the weekend to catch up on sleep.' Now she was becoming boring. Though it wasn't boredom rippling through her body as the impact of that smile continued blasting her. Since when did Raphael's smiles disturb her in any way? Isabella had no answer so went with devouring her now cold pie. Their relationship was changing. Hopefully for the better.

'Have you made appointments to look at flats yet?' No grin now. More of an intense scrutiny of the bottom of his empty mug.

So he wanted her gone sooner than later. Her shoulders slumped. She hauled them tight. She would not be upset. 'I've hardly had time,' she snapped. 'I didn't think there was that much of a hurry.'

'There isn't.' Now he locked eyes with her. 'I just thought you were in a hurry to get started on settling down.'

'Should've known.' She'd reacted too quickly and come up with the wrong answer. 'I'll get on to it shortly. I need to decide where to live that's not too far from the hospital and yet in a bit of a community. If that's possible close to the city centre. I do like the area you're in but rentals there are probably exorbitant. You wouldn't want me too close keeping an eye on what you get up to either.'

He stood and gathered his plate and mug. 'Not true, Izzy. I'm thrilled you're staying in my house, and about to start working on my ward. It's been too long since we spent time together, and we mustn't let that happen again.'

Quite the speech. One that sounded false. She didn't fully understand, and suspected there was something more behind the words. But thrilled? Really? Good. Great even. One thing she knew for certain. 'I agree. It's been for ever since we could sit and shoot the breeze.' For some reason the thought of not having Rafe nearby, if not right beside her, was beginning to feel wrong. As if they were meant to be together. The last crust of her pie fell to the plate. She and Raphael? Together? As in a couple? Come on. That's what she'd been avoiding admitting since arriving in London.

'I'll text you when I'm done tonight.' He was smiling, happiness shining out of his cerulean gaze. 'Want me to take your plate, or are you going to finish that pastry?'

Pushing the plate at him she shook her head, and tried to find something to say. But nothing sensible came up, so she remained quiet. She was off balance, and Raphael wasn't helping by looking at her like he wanted more from her. They knew each other inside out. Ah, not quite. See? She'd never have thought that before. Okay, but since when hadn't she been able to read whatever he wasn't saying? Usually she could do it with her eyes shut. Not today. 'I'll see you later,' she muttered. Yes, she still wanted to have dinner with him. More than before. Really? Yes, really. As in more than catching up. As in getting to know him when she already did. As in trying to understand why she was so off centre around him. Was she on the rebound from Darren? But if this was a rebound, why pick her friend?

Because he's safe and kind and I know where I stand with him.

Oh. That was a wet blanket smothering her. If she did fall in love again, it would be for the right reasons.

I never truly fell completely in love in the first place.

Anyway, no rebound in sight. She was totally over the man. He wasn't as sexy as

Raphael, nor as kind and selfless, or as gorgeous.

Shoving upright, Isabella headed for the exit. The cafeteria had become too small and airless. A few minutes alone outdoors might help unscramble her mind. Might not, either, but she had to try.

'Where are you headed now?' Raphael stood beside her as she peered left, then right.

'Thought I might go introduce myself to the rest of the gang on the ward.' So much for heading outside. She turned in the direction of the lift bank, walked away.

'Isabella.'

She stopped, turned back slowly. 'Yes?'

'This is going to work out for you.' His smile was fleeting, as if not quite believing what he'd said, or not accepting she'd meant it about stopping moving around.

'I hope so.'

Doubtful he heard her quiet reply as he strode away, hands at his sides, back ramrod straight, head up. In Raphael coping mode. What was he coping with? Her decision to live in London? Did he want her here? Or gone by sunrise? He'd suggested she move across the world. Had he changed his mind now it was real? Who knew? She certainly didn't. She needed to get over herself. His mind was more likely to be on his patients, particularly the woman with secondary cancers.

Yet there was a nagging sensation going on at the back of her head saying there was more to this. Isabella slumped against the wall, out of the way of people charging in both directions like they were on missions she was not party to. What was happening to her and Raphael? To their easy, accepting friendship? Never before had she felt awkward with him, yet right now she had no idea what he was thinking or wanting, and that'd happened a few times over the past couple of days.

Her phone rang as she reached the nurses' station on the maternity ward. 'Hello, this is Isabella Nicholson.'

'Jacki Jones, Isabella. I'm ringing to ask a favour.'

Isabella glanced around, saw a woman talking into a phone not more than two metres away. Holding the phone against her chest, she called, 'Jacki? I'm Isabella.'

The head nurse spun around on her chair. 'Oh, hi.' She shoved the phone on its stand and stood to meet her. 'Talk about timely.'

'I've finished the safety course and thought I'd drop by to introduce myself.'

'I was ringing to see if you'd mind starting earlier than first agreed. Tomorrow? We're down on staff and it's bedlam in here.' She had a strong Welsh accent, making Isabella smile. She also seemed to be holding her breath.

Glad of Raphael's warning, the answer came easily. 'Not a problem. Whichever shift you need me on.'

'Thank you.' Jacki's relief was loud and clear. 'Raphael said you probably wouldn't mind, but I still worried you'd say no. It's a bit desperate up here at the moment.'

'Do you want me to put in a few hours this afternoon? I'm signed off on the course and all set to go.'

'Thank you again, but we'll manage today. I know it's only been a couple of days since you arrived in town. Go home and make the most of your time off. You'll be busy enough tomorrow.'

Since her head was starting to pound, she agreed. 'You're probably right.'

A nurse stuck her head around a corner. 'Jacki, I need you in here with Rosalie.' She sounded desperate.

'Coming,' Jacki said calmly. 'A very prem birth, twelve weeks early,' she told Isabella before heading away. 'Raphael's on his way and everything's under control.'

And I'm in the way. Totally get it.

'I'll see you at seven tomorrow.'

'Thanks again, Isabella. I really appreciate it,' Jacki called over her shoulder.

Waiting for the lift again, Isabella texted Carly.

Want a coffee when you knock off?

Not expecting an immediate answer, since Carly was working, she headed for the main entrance and the fresh air. Talking with Carly and hearing more about the man she'd fallen in love with would put everything into perspective, and she'd be able to see Raphael as she'd always done. The best friend ever, who had her back, and had once told her they could rely on each other for anything any time.

Ping. A text landed in her phone.

Three-thirty at the café left of the hospital. Casper's.

Oh, yay. Awesome. Isabella's step picked up as she walked outside. Now what? Nearly an hour to fill in. She'd go for a walk along the Thames and soak up the atmosphere. Stop worrying about everything. Seemed lately she made problems out of anything. Especially her and Raphael. Like she was looking for trouble, when nothing had changed. But it had. She was different. She'd made a serious decision to move here.

You did it in a blink when Raphael made the suggestion.

Raphael. Everything came back to him. She needed to get to the bottom of these niggling concerns, and the sooner, the better. Needed to relax and be happy, more like.

The sun was weak but it didn't matter, the air so much better than the overheated hospital rooms and corridors. The sky was blue with a smattering of fluffy clouds, while boats of all shapes and sizes were making their way purposefully up and down the flowing waters of the Thames. Already there were lots of tourists on the pathways and bridges, cameras busy, selfies being snapped, excitement high, voices loud and excited. This was London. She recalled the first time she'd come here and feeling exactly the same. Hugging herself, she smiled widely at the scene before her and relaxed. The thumping in her head began quietening down.

Strolling along amongst the tourists, hearing a babble of languages and laughter, she let the city take over and push aside everything bothering her, and went with the flow of people all around her. For the first time since landing at Heathrow she didn't feel like falling asleep on her feet despite only a short time ago wanting to crawl into bed, and the

tightness in her belly that had been plaguing
her had taken a hike.

Isabella lost track of time and had to scramble to get back to the café before Carly gave
up on her and headed away. If she hadn't already. Staring around the crowded café she
couldn't see her friend.

'Isabella, Izzy, here.'

Relief and excitement had her charging
through the spaces between the tables to
where Carly stood waving from a table.

Laughing, she reached Carly and was instantly wrapped in a tight hug with a baby
bump in the middle. 'It's been a long time.'

'Hello, you,' Carly murmured against her.

'Blimey, this is amazing. I've missed you
guys so much.'

'Know what you mean.' Carly stepped back
and sank onto a chair, her hand doing a loop
of her belly. 'There's so much to talk about.
First, go grab yourself a coffee. I had to get
my mint tea when I got here so we could have
this table.'

When Isabella returned, with an overfilled
mug and a bottle of water, Carly was texting,

but put her phone aside at once, her face all soft. 'Adem.'

'Look at you. All loved up. I'm so happy for you.' They should've been celebrating with wine, but with a baby in the mix this was the next best thing, as was the talk and laughter as they caught up on day-to-day news. Then Isabella said, 'Tell me all about Adem. When am I going to meet him?'

'Not telling all.' Carly chuckled. 'Izzy, he's everything I've ever wanted and more.'

'As is obvious from your face.' As her friend talked nonstop about her man and the baby they'd made, a mix of happiness for her and an unknown longing for herself rolled through her. 'I am so happy for you. Look at you. You're sparkling.'

'Isn't it great?' Then Carly's perpetual smile dipped. 'How are you now? Completely over that jerk?'

'Have been since the day I caught him out with one of his floozies.' Again, there were things that this close friend didn't have to know. She'd told Raphael in the end, because he was too perceptive for his own good, and she hadn't wanted it hanging between them. Didn't mean Carly needed to learn how stupid she'd been.

'Honestly?'

'Yeah, honestly.'

'Great.' Carly eyeballed her. 'You up for finding another man to have in your life yet? A hot doc, maybe?'

'You're rushing me.' Raphael was as hot as they came. And a doc. Her cup hit the table hard. Can't be. Other women said that about him, not her. Even thinking it was beyond weird.

'I know. I haven't forgotten what it's like to have the man you think you love turn out to be different to your expectations. But I've moved on, and definitely for the better. I only want the same for you.'

'Thanks.' It was a kind thing for Carly to say and it had the longing expanding, had her being truthful. 'Yes, I do eventually want to try again at marriage.' Despite trying to convince herself otherwise. She wanted to fall head over heels in love and not come up for air for a long time. 'This time with someone who doesn't stray.' Raphael would never do that. Gasp. The cup shook when she picked it up again. What was going on? Her head was all over the place. Couldn't blame this on the long-haul flight. She was the problem. Or Raphael.

'How's Raphael? It's cool that you're staying with him.' Then Carly took on a surprised look. 'Raphael's single. You get on brilliantly with him. Now there's a thought. I can see that working.'

'Carly,' Isabella snapped. 'Stop right there. We are friends,' she ground out, not liking how Carly had come to a similar conclusion she was working her way towards. 'You know, as in talk, and laugh, and do things together, but not have sex or kiss. Or set up house and have babies.' Who was she trying to convince here?

Carly merely laughed. 'You think? He's hot, knows you inside out. Okay, not quite, but that can easily be fixed. Seriously, what's wrong with the idea?'

'Everything.' Nothing. Her fingers trembled, her head spun. No way. This conversation was not happening. 'You're doing what everyone who's just fallen in love does— trying to set up your single friends to have the same experience.'

'Too right. And Raphael's perfect for you. The whole situation's perfect. You're living in his house, spending lots of time with him. Make it happen, Izzy. Can you honestly say you haven't looked at him as other women do and gone, wow, he's gorgeous?'

That *perfect* word again. Better get on the phone to make appointments with the letting agents ASAP. Except when could she find time to go looking when she was starting a new job tomorrow, and needed to see the dressmaker for a fitting for her bridesmaid dress, and still got tired without trying? She refused to think about putting this other aberration to bed. Alone. 'I haven't,' she muttered. It used to be true. Not so long ago in the cafeteria she'd noted how well he filled out his suit. Friends didn't do that. Did they? She hadn't in the past. Damn, this was getting too complicated. So much for relaxing with Carly. Now she was wound up tighter than ever. 'Concentrate on Adem and leave my life to me.'

Carly's reply to that was to laugh.

'Thanks, friend.' After this conversation it was apparent she'd have to be wary about how often she mentioned Raphael. Couldn't have Carly keeping an eye on her and Rafe to see if there was anything growing between them. Oh, damn, he was going to the wedding with her.

The moment Isabella sat down beside Raphael in the pub she'd agreed to meet him at after she'd said goodbye to Carly, any thought of moving vamoosed. Only to return when she realised he was hardly talking. But why rush into any old flat just to put space between them when they got along so well? Except they weren't so easy with each other at the moment. Okay, she'd make time to visit the rental agencies. In the meantime staying with him might fix this strange idea he meant something else to her now from expanding further. They'd inevitably quarrel over the dishes left in the sink or about one of them emptying the milk and not replacing it. That's what flatmates did. It was normal. It would ground her in reality. Or it could grow, expand, take over her common sense.

'Here, you look like you need this.'

She grabbed the wineglass Raphael was holding out to her, took a mouthful. 'Thanks.' The wine was cold, and calming. She took a breath, had another mouthful, felt the tension begin to ebb away. 'I see you're on the lemonade.'

'The joys of being on call.' He settled more comfortably on his stool. A good sign. 'I hear you've agreed to start tomorrow.'

'Jacki talked to me briefly this afternoon—when she wasn't running round like a headless chook. The ward was frantic.'

'Don't call her that to her face, or she'll put you on cleaning bedpans for a week.'

'Not the nurse I saw talking about a woman who'd gone into labour twelve weeks early. She seemed so calm, while a few doors away the woman was crying loud enough to be heard all over the hospital.'

'The baby came in a hell of a hurry and is

now in PICU, attached to every monitor ever invented. Joseph Raphael Gleeson. Fitted into my hand like a newborn puppy when I transferred him to the incubator.' Rafe held up his hand. 'Doesn't matter how often I deliver these prem babies, I never get used to that. If all goes well, one day he'll be an adult, working, playing, maybe having his own kids.'

'A puppy? You and your dogs. Better keep *that* to yourself or no one will want you near their babies.' Isabella laughed. Placing her hand on his, she squeezed gently, her eyes watering. 'They named him after you. That's cool. Bet it gave you hiccups when they told you.'

'It did. Apparently Joseph, his grandfather, is thrilled too.' Raphael turned his hand over and wound his fingers between hers.

Oops. Bad move. She carefully extracted her fingers. 'How many Raphaels are out there because of you?'

'Not too many, *merci*. Imagine if I'd been given a really horrible name. There'd be all these poor little blighters cowering at the school gates every day, waiting for the teasing to begin.'

She laughed again, and withdrew her hand. Reluctantly, she realised with a jolt. 'I can't think of any names that bad.' They'd briefly held hands. As in how friends didn't do. More laughter bubbled to the fore. She held it in, afraid Raphael would want to know what was funny. Happiness wasn't funny, and she'd swear she was very happy, happier than she'd been in ages. Did Carly have a point? More to think about. Later. When she was tucked up in bed—on her own. What? As if anyone would be with her. Her gaze flicked to the man sitting with her. This was becoming beyond bizarre. And yet the happiness still bubbled through her.

Raphael was doing that staring into the bottom of his drink trick again. It happened quite a lot. 'I'm attending a conference in Cardiff this weekend. Won't be around to take you shopping.'

'As if I need you for that. I do know my way around. I'm also hoping to look at a couple of flats on Saturday morning. The woman I dealt with from Wellington rang to say she had some places that might work for me.'

That could not be disappointment flickering across his face. 'That's quick.'

'Yes, well, don't want to hang around harassing you for too long. You might regret getting me the job and I need it.'

'Don't go making any decisions that you'll regret later.'

'I'll run everything by you if I find a place I like.'

'Do that.'

'I got a text from Jacki an hour ago, asking if I'd fill in on Saturday night. I said yes.'

'There's no holding you back, is there?' Raphael sipped his drink. 'Let's order. I've got some notes to go over when I get home.'

'For the conference?'

He nodded. 'On Sunday morning, along with the man who still mentors me, I'm speaking about two cases of early menopause we had this year.' A wry smile crossed his mouth. 'Not sure why he wanted me there, since most things that will come out of my mouth came from him in the first place.'

'Is that what you were doing in your office late last night? Working on your talk?' She'd gone downstairs for a glass of water and seen Raphael hunched over his computer, completely focused on the screen. 'You looked like nothing could interrupt you.'

'Obviously you didn't.' He grinned.

'You know me, quiet as a mouse.' Looking around, she noted the place was filling up. 'Want to share a pizza? I don't want to be out late either. Starting a new job in the morning, you know.'

Raphael couldn't forget that if he wanted to. He'd spent the night tossing and turning, thinking about Isabella and their relationship. So much for wishing for her to come to London, and to work with him. He'd got what he'd asked for all right, he groaned as he snapped off the vinyl gloves he wore and dropped them in the theatre's bin.

At 6:10 they'd caught the same train into the hospital, Izzy up early and ready to go long before he'd got his act together. She'd even looked more focused than he'd felt. But the usual evidence of her not getting through the night without going down to the kitchen had been there when he'd finally made it to the coffee machine—all primed and ready to share its life-saving liquid. Maybe she hadn't gone to bed at all.

His work phone buzzed. It was Jacki. Can you look in on Milly Frost sooner than later?

So he wasn't going to avoid seeing Izzy throughout the day. Not that he could avoid going on the ward for eight hours, but thankfully surgery had kept him busy until now. 'So much for lunch,' he muttered as he dried his hands and checked his tie in the mirror.

'Should've studied grass growing if you wanted meals at set hours,' one of the theatre nurses quipped.

'See you back here, hopefully on time,' he threw over his shoulder as he headed out of the theatre suite.

'Isabella noticed the foetal heart rate's stressed,' the head nurse explained when he strode into Milly's room. 'I've checked and agree.'

Jacki would've been keeping a close eye on

everything Isabella did today. It was always a strain taking on new staff, no matter how highly recommended they came. Raphael nodded. 'I'll listen to the heartbeat as well.' Three heads were better than one. Finding a smile he turned to his patient. 'Hello, Milly. Aaron.' He nodded at the woman's husband. 'I understand your labour is going well, but baby might be distressed. I'm going to listen to the heart and watch the screen here to get a clear picture of what's happening.' If Isabella and Jacki were correct, he and Milly would be going to Theatre shortly, and as those two nurses were good at what they did, and wouldn't have made a mistake, he had an unexpected operation ahead of him. Nothing unusual in that, just meant he'd be later getting home. Again, nothing unusual, but for the first time in years, he regretted it.

Thought you were wanting time away from Izzy?

Face it. He didn't have a clue what he wanted.

'Is Evie going to be all right?' Fear darkened Milly's eyes as she scrabbled around for Aaron's hand.

Milly's question put him back on track. 'Let's see what's happening before I answer that.'

On the other side of the bed Isabella was lifting back the sheet in preparation to pull Milly's gown up and expose her baby tummy. Then, 'Another contraction, Milly?' As their patient rocked forward, pain marring her face and tightening her grip on her husband's hand, Isabella rubbed her back and waited for the spasm to pass.

Raphael also waited, watching the screen on the foetal heart rate monitor. Thankfully baby's heart rate did not slow any further during the contraction so no recovery afterwards, but it was already too slow and the contraction had done nothing to alter what was going on with baby. Next he listened through his stethoscope. 'Has baby been moving as much as usual?'

'Not for the last little while,' Milly cried. 'I didn't say anything. I thought he was rest-ing. We've been going at this for a few hours now. It's all my fault.'

'It's nobody's fault.' Had there been any indicators he should've seen earlier? Before labour started? No. He knew there weren't, and playing the blame game did no one any favours. 'I see Isabella's noted he slowed down very recently.' He straightened up and delivered the news Milly and Aaron would not want to hear. Even though saving their daughter's life was the priority this wasn't how they'd planned on welcoming their baby into the world. 'I'm going to do a C-section. Baby's distressed and it isn't safe to leave her in there.'

'Is Evie going to be all right?' Milly repeated, this time with fear echoing around the room.

'Is our daughter in danger?' Aaron shouted.

This never got any easier. 'Surgery is the safest option. There's some risk of meconium being in the amniotic fluid. I don't want her breathing that in, so urgency is required. Isabella will prepare you to go down to Theatre, while I go organise the emergency team and scrub up, Milly.' He paused for a moment, fully expecting a load of questions, but the parents were both stunned—gripping their joined hands and staring at each other in raw silence. 'Isabella—' he nodded '—stay with Milly and Aaron until they go into Theatre.' Then he was striding away, talking on his phone to the head theatre nurse. 'My next procedure has changed. Urgent C-section to save full-term baby.'

'Do you want to cancel any surgery on this afternoon's list?' Kelly was very matter of fact. No wasting time on trivia.

'Not at this point. Let's see how we go.' Which meant he'd do all the listed procedures. Cancelling an operation was hard on patients when they were mentally prepared to go under the knife. He reached the scrub room and began preparing, his mind busy with every step of the procedure he'd done innumerable times. Milly and Aaron's daughter was going to get every chance on offer and more.

Evie Frost was delivered within minutes of Milly reaching Theatre. Raphael checked her breathing for abnormalities, and gave the mother a smile. 'All good. No meconium in her lungs.' Relief thumped behind his ribs. 'Evie's heart rate's normal for all she's been through.' He watched as a nurse handed Milly her daughter, and felt the familiar lump of awe build in his throat. New parenthood was wonderful, special. There weren't enough words to describe the amazement covering mums' and dads' faces when they met their child for the first time. Aaron was looking gobsmacked. Love spilled out of his gaze as he stared at his wife and daughter.

Raphael moved away. Despite how often he'd witnessed that scene it never grew stale. The awe he'd known the day Pierre slid into his shaking hands had never left him. That tiny boy had grown into a wonderful, strong lad with a great enthusiasm for life and an abundance of confidence. Raphael felt proud for being a part of his arrival, although he'd actually done little more than make his cousin comfortable and catch Pierre as he shot out into the world.

'Well done.' Kelly walked alongside him.

'Thanks. He's a little beauty.' He'd done a good job for baby and parents. Then the usual flip side of the euphoria hit. Anger filled him. What about *his* baby? What had he looked like? Who did he follow? Blond or dark? Short or tall? Cassie had refused to tell him anything, saying it was best he didn't know. Best for who? She'd never answered that question. He spun away, headed for the lift. He needed air and no friendly faces while he swallowed this particular pill yet again.

Then he'd return to Theatre and lose himself in work.

When Raphael called in on Milly after his last operation for the day Isabella was there. 'Evie's so cute. But then I say that about them all.' She'd been keeping a close eye on mum and baby all afternoon.

Now she and Raphael moved out of the little room to stand in the corridor. 'You ever think about having your own brood?' It was one thing Izzy had never talked about. Probably because it hadn't been an issue until she'd married Darren and then he hadn't wanted to hear her say yes. As for him, yes, he'd wanted children. Still did, but… Joshua, his little boy he'd never met… How did he cope with getting someone pregnant and waiting out the nine months until he got to hold his child? He was watching Izzy, wondering what she would say even as he dealt with his own pain.

She blinked, appeared to think about it. 'I've always presumed I would one day, and thought it would come about when I married. Now, I can't say I've been planning on it happening any time soon, if at all. It's filed with other things I hope to get to do some time, and when I do, be grateful if all goes according to plan.'

In this job they saw enough times when people's dreams of having a family went horribly wrong to know there were no guarantees. But was she referring to that, or her expectations for her future? Not asking. Not here anyway. 'What will be, will be,' he quoted.

Isabella nodded. 'Everyone thinks it's a given we'll get pregnant when we want to, but working in this job I've learnt how wrong that assumption can be.' Then she shrugged and perked up. 'We're being glum when there's a very lucky little girl in there with two of the happiest people in the world.'

'True. Weren't you meant to knock off an hour ago?' He still had patients to see, but surgery was finished, and suddenly he was exhausted. That often happened after a big day in Theatre and on the ward. Especially after a sleepless night. Add in the confusion Izzy was causing him and he was screwed. 'Feel like picking up some Italian on the way home? I'll be at least another hour.'

'I'll get the take-out and see you at home.'

At home. A soft sigh escaped.

If only you knew, Isabella Nicholson.

Putting his hand in his pocket for his wallet, he smiled when she shook her head.

'My shout.'

'Fair enough.' He knew better than to argue. He wouldn't win. 'See you later.' The sooner he checked on his patients, the sooner he could go home. Home. The connotations of that word had never been so huge. So frightening. Yet the need to settle grew the more time he spent with Isabella. She wasn't the only one wanting to find that special place in life. At least she'd made a start at getting on with it. Wouldn't it be great if he and Izzy could get what they wanted—together?

Stop right there. She's been hurt once. You can't risk putting her through that again.

No, he couldn't. It was his role as a friend to keep her safe, which meant putting some barriers up between them.

CHAPTER SIX

'THANK GOODNESS FOR FRIDAYS.' Isabella slammed the front door shut and stared along the hallway.

'You didn't even do a full week,' Raphael called from the kitchen at the far end. 'Come on. I've been waiting for you to get home so we can have a drink.'

'Good idea.' She was entitled to one after the hectic few days she'd spent on the ward.

'Dinner's not far off.' Raphael's glass of red wine with dinner was a nightly ritual. Another French habit he'd picked up from his family back in Avignon.

At the door into the kitchen she paused, gazed at Rafe as he stirred a sauce in a pot while at the same time squeezing garlic into it. She hadn't seen him so relaxed. It suited him. 'That smells divine.' Beat take-out any night of the week.

'Boeuf Bordelaise.'

'Yum.' So was the sight before her. 'What happened to heading to Cardiff today? Isn't that why you took the afternoon off?'

His shrug was a little stiff. Not so relaxed now she was here? 'No rush. The conference proper doesn't start till nine tomorrow. I'll head away first in the morning. Won't miss much if I'm a bit late.'

Warmth filled her. It wouldn't be a night alone after all. 'Cool. I'll get changed.' That wine was sounding better and better. She'd spent an hour with Carly, discussing the wedding, and love. She'd mostly listened, trying to ignore the flare of sadness that she wouldn't be walking down another aisle any time soon. There'd also been her selfish wish that Carly didn't have a man to rush home to, could go out on the town with her. But deep down, she was more than happy for her friend, and got over her funk quickly.

Up three stairs and she hesitated. Again it felt as though the ceiling was coming down on top of her and the walls crowding in. 'That colour has got to go.' Or she was more tired than she'd realised. She headed upward again, in a hurry to get away from the darkness.

'Izzy?' Raphael had come along the hall and was looking up at her. 'What are you on about?'

'That magenta is hideous. It's so dark and brooding, makes the hall seem smaller than it really is.' Not even the cream paint of the stair rails softened the atmosphere, instead accentuated all that was wrong with the paintwork.

He shrugged. 'Like I said the other day, changing it is on the list. I just don't happen to have forty-eight hours in every day.'

'When you've poured that wine can you get out the colour schemes you said came with the place?' Not waiting for an answer, she continued upstairs.

'Oui, madame.'

They'd never got around to the French week, but it didn't really matter since they flipped from English to French and back again all the time.

Pausing, she looked back down at Raphael.

'I have more free time than you, and I like re-decorating.' She could help until she moved. When she found some free time that was. 'I'll wow you with my skills.'

'Oh, no. You are not going to paint my hall-way.'

'Why not? It's not like I haven't done this sort of thing before.' Being useful, instead of feeling a bit redundant, might help her sleep at night, too. 'Find those charts.'

His mouth twitched. 'You know how to make a man feel guilty.'

He had to be pulling her leg. He'd be more than happy to have the *problem* taken out of his hands, and having her do that shouldn't be getting him in a twist. 'You can't come up with a reason for me not to do it, can you?' Fist pumping the air, she grinned. 'Love it when I win.'

Raphael shook his head at her before head-ing back down the hall.

There was a small pile of charts on the table when she returned showered and in clean clothes. 'What are these?' she asked, tapping some pages of notes.

'The interior design suggestions that came with the house. Like I said, I'm not the only one who hasn't got around to doing up this place.'

'It's not everyone's idea of fun,' she conceded, flicking through the pages and pausing at a design for a new kitchen layout. 'Wow, I like this.' Glancing around the kitchen, she nodded. 'Lighter for one. Far more functional for another. And modern.'

'That's not hard to achieve when you think how old this must be.' Raphael was also staring around, looking as though he'd never really seen it before. 'I wonder if the design company's still got the in-depth plans?' Excitement was beginning to crowd his gaze. 'They're based on the other side of Richmond.'

'Only one way to find out,' she drawled.

He grinned and pushed her glass in front of her. 'Drink up and stop being annoying.'

'Why is wanting to help being annoying?' The wine was delicious, a perfect end to a busy day.

Ignoring her question, he went with some

of his own. 'How do you feel after your first week on the maternity ward? Glad you joined us?' He gave the sauce a stir before leaning against the counter and stretching his legs before him. Legs that went on for ever.

Gulp. He'd always had those legs. Why were they any different tonight? Another gulp of wine. What was the question? Oh, right. 'I'm loving it. And yes, I believe it was the right move. Though only time will really be the judge of that.' Following his example, she perched on another chair and reached for the colour charts, noting the ones that had been circled with a marker pen.

'I'll add my bit to making it happen.'

'Tell me something I don't know. You'll be a dog with a bone.' Looking around she spied Chienne on her cushion. 'Sorry, not trying to insult you, Cat. You're too good for bones.' The cat was getting to her, making her feel more and more at ease. But then she did like to share the bed in the darkest hours of the night, or curl up on her lap when she came downstairs for a glass of water and some upright time in an attempt to get into a fall-asleep zone.

'Don't listen to her, Chienne. Izzy likes to con everyone round to her way of thinking.'

'Why not if it gets me what I want?' She grinned. Then focused on the colours that had been circled with a marker pen, rather than stare at those thighs filling his black jeans. 'Who suggested these colours?' They weren't bad. The colours? Or the thighs? She could live with them. Both of them. Gulp. Nice wine. Hope there was more in that bottle for after dinner.

'Believe it or not, in the first months when I was fired up to get on with fixing the place up I visited the paint shop and the woman I spoke to was very helpful with suggestions. Said these were the latest in colour schemes and if I want to sell the place would appeal to more buyers.'

'You're thinking of moving? Already?' First she'd heard of it. She didn't like it. She was getting used to Raphael being here and had hoped they'd live in the same vicinity long term. Was he really considering moving again? Of course she'd known he would eventually return to Avignon. That's why. He'd always felt a pull towards his family and hometown. As she had with Wellington. Look where that got her. It hadn't been Wellington at fault, more her and the man she'd returned there with. Whereas Avignon might very well be the best thing for Raphael. Her heart stuttered. Didn't she want him to be happy? Deep, deep breath. Yes, she did. More than anything. More than her own happiness. Truly? A sip of wine. Truly.

'Can't guarantee anything's for ever. But I'm here for the foreseeable future at least.' He spaced the words, loud and clear, as though it was important she believed him.

The relief was strong. 'Glad to hear it.'

'What are you looking for in a flat?' He sipped his drink as he waited for her reply.

'Two bedrooms, though I guess one would suffice. Located near a train station, of course, and close to shops and food outlets.'

'Sounds ordinary.'

'I guess it is, but ordinary's fine for now.'

'As long as it doesn't bore you, Izzy.'

'I'm not about to dash away again. This is a permanent move. I'm determined to keep it that way.'

Raphael went back to stirring his sauce. 'You ever feel it's not working out please tell me.'

'Why?' The word shot out of her mouth.

Tipping his head back, he stared up at the ceiling.

And she waited, sensing if she uttered one word he'd not answer her.

Finally his head dropped forward, and he took a small mouthful of his merlot. 'I like having you back in London.'

So? She liked being here. But was that what this was about? She waited, breath caught in her throat.

His words were measured as he continued. 'I've lived here for two years, and when I say lived I mean I've come and gone, and not really noticed the place. It is four walls and shelter, comfortable in a less than desirable way. It's a house, not a home.'

What did that have to do with her?

'Since you arrived, it already feels different, more like the home I intended making it. *My* home. I think about coming back at the end of the day now, not just going somewhere to eat, shower, study and sleep.' He stopped.

What to say to that? Her mouth had dried, and there didn't seem to be any answers forthcoming to what Raphael had just said. Inside, that feeling of finally getting her life right expanded a wee bit more. They did fit well together, but how well? Were they becoming more than friends? Was that even wise given there'd been no attraction in the past? Could people suddenly want someone physically after spending most of their lives not noticing each other that way? 'I'm glad you're finally enjoying your home.'

Crass, Izzy, crass.

Totally. But she couldn't tell him what she'd been thinking. For one, she hadn't been here very long, and secondly, she had to haul on the brakes. She wasn't reliable in relationships, and Raphael was vulnerable after how Cassie dumped him.

'I've surprised you.' Raphael was studying her.

What was that about? 'A little.' It would be a relief to tell him how she felt, but then there'd be a whole other can of worms to deal with. Best shut up. She began flicking through paint charts, the colours one big blur as thoughts of holding Raphael, of kissing him, being kissed back, rose and heated her before she could squash them back in place.

At five next morning, fifteen minutes before the alarm was due to go off, Raphael dragged himself out of bed and into the shower, then stared at his puffy face in the mirror as he shaved.

'Don't lose any sleep over where I'll find a place to live,' Izzy had said over their beef dinner. How prophetic.

She'd blighted his night with thoughts of what it might be like if she didn't find a flat, and instead stayed on with him, moved down to the second floor and his bedroom. Of course none of that had been suggested, but he hadn't been able to think of anything else as he'd watched her swing her small but shapely legs while she sat on the stool. The relief had been immense when he'd put dinner on the table and she'd had to shift. But then he'd been subjected to seeing her fork food through those full lips, and conjuring up thoughts of her mouth on his skin.

The razor slipped. He swore. Dabbed the blood away. 'Concentrate, man.' Hell, now she had him talking to himself like some brain-dead moron on P.

It was far easier to blame Isabella than take a long, serious look at himself. If he did that, he'd have to admit he was floundering here, and hell, he didn't usually get into a quagmire over his own emotions when it came to women. Only Cassie had done that to him. Until now. Now Izzy was having a damned good go at tipping him upside down. At least she was on the good side of the barometer, not like the hellhole Cassie had shoved him into. But then it was not as though he was falling hard for Izzy like he had for Cassie. If anything he was getting there slowly, carefully, and with a whole heap of concerns to deal with.

Focusing entirely on removing the last of

the growth on his face, he managed to quieten his thumping chest for a few minutes. No more nicks on his skin. Yet the moment he rinsed the shaver the thumping started up again. This strange sensation Izzy brought on threw him whenever he wasn't totally engrossed in work or study or any other blasted thing that didn't start with *I*. He couldn't go on ignoring his feelings for her. Nor could he do a thing about it until he returned from Cardiff. Taking a mug of coffee up to her room and saying, 'Oh, by the way, I think I might want to spend the rest of my life with you. Can't talk now. Lots to sort out first. See you tomorrow night,' wouldn't win him any favours. Not that he had worked out how to approach this yet, only understood the time was coming when he'd not be able to stay uninvolved. All he knew was if Izzy laughed at him, he'd die inside.

Now his alarm woke him up. As in out of his stupor and into getting ready for the trip to Wales. Swiping the screen of his phone to shut the infernal noise off, he tossed it into his overnight bag along with his shaving gear, and got dressed in his latest swanky suit and tie. Bag zipped shut, he headed downstairs for a quick coffee and toast before hitting the road. He was early due to that lack of sleep, but hopefully that meant the roads would have less traffic to contend with.

'Hey, coffee's ready and waiting. I put it on when I heard you moving around up there.' Izzy sat at the round table at the edge of the kitchen, a mug in one hand, and Chienne on her lap schmoozing against her other hand.

'Morning.' He hadn't smelt a thing. Too distracted. Then, 'Cheeky.' He nodded at the cat. 'You'll do anything to get attention.' He wouldn't ogle Isabella in her sleeveless top with no bra underneath. Was that a pyjama top? Guess so, if the matching loose shorts Chienne was stretched across were an indicator. So she—Izzy, not Chienne—still wore shapeless PJs. Or had she reverted to them once Darren had left the scene? He'd seen enough on washing lines throughout their lives to know she'd never been one for matching bras and knickers, let alone fancy lingerie of any kind, but who knew what being in a relationship might've done for her? Turning away, his mind filled with an image of her in black sexy lingerie. And he swore.

'Pardon?'

Did he say that out loud? Sloshing coffee into the mug waiting by the coffee machine, he drew a slow breath and looked over his shoulder. 'Sorry. I spilled coffee, that's all.' Grabbing a cloth he made a show of wiping down the bench, which was coffee-free. If this was what not sleeping did to him, then how did Izzy manage day to day on the little she got?

'I take it you didn't sleep again? Perhaps you should stop drinking coffee.'

'One step ahead of you.' She waved her mug at him. 'This is tea. Not that I'm giving up entirely on my caffeine fix.'

Then he noticed the paint charts once again spread over the table. Showed how much attention he'd been paying to Izzy and her PJs if he hadn't seen those. 'You are serious about getting the decorating under way, aren't you?'

A rare worry flickered through her eyes. 'Does that bother you?'

He shook his head. 'Not at all. I should've known you'd get stuck into sorting my mess out.' It was what she'd always done. Only difference was this was a large, hands-on job, not like making sure the rowdy guys in the room next door at university stopped banging on his door in the middle of the night when he was trying to study.

Her shoulders softened, and Chienne got another stroke. Lucky cat. 'It's okay. You'll recognise the house when you return tomorrow night. I've got too much else on today.'

'Thank goodness for that,' he retorted. 'Can't have you taking over completely.' The coffee was blistering hot and he needed to be on the road. 'I'll put this in a travel mug. Got to go.'

'Fine.' Izzy sipped her tea. When her tongue did a lap of her lips the thumping started up in his chest again, only harder and faster.

Just as well he was going away.

Except as Raphael and his colleague, Jeremy, stood onstage receiving a hearty round of applause at the end of their talk on Sunday, he knew he wasn't hanging around for the afternoon's workshops. 'I'm out of here,' he muttered in an aside.

'I'm not surprised. You've been miles away since you got here. Except during our talk,' Jeremy added hastily.

'It's a miracle I managed to get through that without making stuff up.' Though he had concentrated hard, determined Isabella wasn't going to wreck everything about this weekend. He missed her. Had done from the moment he'd backed out onto the road in Richmond yesterday morning. It had taken strength not to text to see what she was up to. He just wanted to be with her, even when that twisted his gut and tightened muscles best ignored. Sure, he wouldn't be able to do what he really wanted to—kiss those tantalising lips and hold that soft, curvy body against him—but he could give her cheek and laugh, and make her a mug of tea.

'What's playing on your mind?' Jeremy asked as they stepped offstage.

'Nothing to do with work,' Raphael was quick to reassure his mentor.

'I didn't think so.'

Right. Now what? He hated lying to anyone, and particularly to this man who'd been nothing but kind and helpful to him from the day they met in the gynaecology department when he'd come on board as the newest specialist. 'Just some personal stuff.' Hopefully Jeremy would get the hint and drop the subject. Not that he'd ever done that if he really felt it important to get to the bottom of something. The man could be a hound when he put his mind to it.

'Woman trouble?'

Got that right. Now what? He wasn't talking about Izzy to anyone. He tried to laugh it off. 'Isn't it always about women?'

'Not with you, my friend. You make sure of that; no repercussions when a fling is over. Everyone comes out smiling. Even you.'

Yes, and could be that was the problem. He had got not getting involved down to a fine art. *Magnifique.* He was getting nowhere fast. Try the truth line again, diluted, of course.

'My close friend Isabella is staying with me at the moment.'

'And you want to get home to spend time with her. Why didn't you say so?' Then Jeremy's eyes widened. 'Oh, oh. I sense trouble.' He tapped Raphael's chest. 'In there.'

'Stick with gynaecology, will you? You're better at it.'

Jeremy didn't laugh. Not even a glimmer of amusement showed in his face. 'This Isabella, I've met her on the ward. She's a very competent midwife. So she's special? You've known her a long time?'

'Since I was an incompetent teen.'

'And now you're not incompetent. Nor do you want to remain just friends.'

Mon amie. Izzy. Special. More than a friend.

Jeremy gripped his arm. 'What are you going to miss by not being here for the rest of the day? Nothing you don't already know. It's time you put your personal life before your career. You need a balanced life, Raphael, one where you have someone to go home with at the end of the day.'

'Don't I know it.' Yet it was a new idea, one that began filling him with hope from the day he'd picked Izzy up at the airport.

No, not new, because two years ago he'd seen what he wanted and had had to bury the longing, to focus on the other thing necessary to him—work. Not Isabella. 'Thanks, Jeremy. I'm out of here.'

Not that he was heading home to spill his heart. No way. There was a lot to work through before he was even close to admitting his love. Time spent with Izzy, laughing and talking, or more likely arguing over next to nothing, was always time well spent. Hopefully he'd be relaxed and she wouldn't pick up on these new feelings because he had to get them under control and back in the box.

The house was locked up when he arrived home. Inside, as he walked along the hall, he called out, 'Izzy? You about?'

Silence greeted him.

The vacuum cleaner stood against the wall, still plugged in, as if Isabella had been interrupted, and fully expected to come back to the job she'd started.

There was no note on the table explaining where she was. Nor on his phone. Not that there should be. She wouldn't have been expecting him home this early, but still. The anticipation that had been growing as he'd negotiated highways and roads filled with weekenders with nothing better to do than get in the way evaporated, leaving him feeling like an idiot. Of course Izzy would be out doing her thing, hadn't been sitting here pining the hours away. Why would she?

He'd text and see where she was. Might go join her for a drink or some shopping or whatever took her fancy. It was yesterday she'd gone to look at flats. Had she found one she liked and gone back for a second look? That could mean she'd be out of here soon and he could get back to his quiet life—which he didn't want any more. Truly? Yes. Didn't mean he knew what he was going to do about it though.

Raphael sighed, then reverted to normal and went in to the Queen Victoria to see how his patients were faring.

'I'll get you a new tumbler,' Isabella told Brooke. 'It's not a problem.' Her patient was stressing out over every little thing as the contractions got harder and closer together.

'You're so calm, it's annoying,' Brooke growled through gritted teeth.

Isabella chuckled. 'You're not the first to complain about that.'

'Wait until you have a baby and then see how composed you are.' The woman blinked. 'Or have you had children of your own?'

'Not yet.'

Not yet? Like there was a possibility in the near future? Raphael flashed across her mind. As he'd been doing all weekend. No wonder she'd agreed immediately when asked to come in and work the afternoon after one of the nurses had gone off with a stomach bug. But Raphael and babies and her? All in the one sentence? As if that was happening. Although they were getting on in a closer way than ever before, and she had no idea where that was leading, there was always an air of uncertainty between them. Besides, her dream of babies with Darren had been stolen from her. She wasn't ready to be that vulnerable again.

'Got to get a man first,' she told Brooke.

But not before I get that tumbler.

Heading for the water dispenser and the stack of plastic mugs, she glanced at her watch. Less than an hour to go. It had been a frantic few hours, babies arriving in all directions.

Raphael had been quiet. No texts asking what she was doing, or telling her how the conference was going. He'd have finished his talk hours ago, could possibly be on the road by now. Wonder what he'd like for dinner?

After giving Brooke her water and checking how baby was doing, Isabella went to see Caitlin Simons, who had delivered an hour ago. Since the door was open she popped her head around the corner of Caitlin's room to make sure she wasn't interrupting anything, and stopped, a gasp whispering across her lips.

Raphael was sitting awkwardly on a narrow chair. Baby Simons swathed in light blankets was cradled in his arms. The usual look of relief was in his gaze as he looked down at the boy, but there was something else too. Something like—pain? But it couldn't be. What was there to be sad about here?

A sharp pain stabbed her chest. A lump blocked her throat. Breathing became difficult. Rafe would make a wonderful father. Despite that intense look there was something so tender about him that blindsided her. Shook her to the core.

She could never imagine Darren like this.

She stared at the beautiful man holding the tiny baby, and the floor moved beneath her feet. The air thickened, breathing became impossible.

This was Rafe, the man she'd known for so long. This was Raphael, a man she'd begun falling in love with. She couldn't do a thing about that because she wasn't settled, could not risk hurting him. Raphael was polar opposite to her ex. How could she have thought she loved Darren? This feeling she'd been denying since arriving in London was so different to anything she'd felt for him. Strong and soft, caring and gentle, hungry and fulfilling.

Isabella closed her eyes, counted to ten, opened them. Her eyes filled with tears. She and Raphael made great friends. What would they be like as lovers? He deserved someone who would stick by him through thick and thin, and she couldn't guarantee that was her, no matter how hard she was trying to settle here. The picture before her would've been perfect if that was their child. As she swiped at her cheeks her heart crashed against her ribs. Now what? How could she return to his house tonight as if nothing had changed? She had to get away. Turning around she froze when Raphael called out.

'Hey, Izzy, come and meet Fleur.' Raphael's eyes locked with hers, nailing her to the spot.

She took an unsteady step, then another, and another, until at last she stood before him and looked down, down at the baby but mostly at Raphael. Saw him as the man she wanted to spend her life with.

'Want a hold?' He lifted the child towards her.

'I've already had a hold.' She took a step back, afraid she'd drop Fleur. Which was plain stupid, considering how many babies she'd held during her career.

'Have another.'

'Okay,' she whispered.

'Come on. She's so cute.' Raphael stood up, held out the precious bundle.

Taking the baby, she stared down at the wrinkly, pink face of the girl she'd help deliver earlier, and who now opened her eyes wide. 'Hello, Fleur.' Then she couldn't say another word, fear of telling Raphael about the mass of emotions tying her in knots.

'Izzy?'

'Isabella, Brooke's asking for you,' Claudia called across the room. 'I don't think we've long to go now.'

'On my way.' Gently placing Fleur back in her bed, she turned to Caitlin. 'She's gorgeous. Well done, you. Anything I can get you?'

'My mum. She's gone for a coffee, and I need her here.' Caitlin was a solo mum, the father having done a bunk when he learned about the pregnancy.

'Not a problem. I'll dash down to the cafeteria right now.' Phew. That'd give her some space from Raphael. 'Make that after I've checked on my other patient.'

'I'll go see Mrs Johnson, Izzy,' Raphael said.

So much for getting away from him while she cleared her head. But what could she say? She might be one of the midwives on the case, but doctors came first. Always. Glancing across at him, she saw he was looking more like his normal self, the longing and awe now under control. 'Fine.'

'How long have you been on shift?' he asked as he made for the door.

'Started around lunchtime, and should be finished shortly.' Not regular shift hours but who cared? If she was needed here, then that was fine by her. Ignoring any further questions Raphael might come up with, she said to Caitlin, 'Fleur's lovely. Thank you for letting me hold her.' Then she shot away to find Mrs Simons, who'd hopefully put a smile back on her daughter's face. It was hard for the women who had to go through labour without their soul mate. A friend or family member was well and good, but not the same thing as a doting husband or partner.

'Isabella, wait.' Raphael was right behind her. 'Are you all right?'

'Yes,' she muttered. 'I got side tracked in there when I should've been with Brooke.' Not that she'd done anything wrong. Brooke had not been ready to give birth when she left the room.

'You find a flat?'

'Yes.' Her mouth was dry, her hands damp. Snatching a plastic cup at the water dispenser she filled it and turned to head for the lift only to come to an abrupt stop in front of Raphael. She couldn't read his expression at all. 'You came back early from Cardiff.'

'I'd had enough of being squashed into the hotel conference room.' His reply was terse.

'Thought you were meant to be getting a life outside these walls.' And who dropped the housework to come in here when Jacki called to say she was desperate for staff for the rest of the day shift? Who hadn't gone home when the next shift arrived?

'I won't hang around after I've seen Brooke.

But first, are you sure you're okay? You looked a tad pale, and are as jumpy as a frog on steroids.' Nothing but concern radiated out of those blue eyes.

Damn it. Think of something to say that'll keep him happy. Think, girl. 'Just didn't expect to see you holding Fleur like you never wanted to let her go, that's all.' Wrong. All wrong, and she couldn't take back a single word.

'What?' Raphael glanced at her. 'Never.'

Shrugging aside her mood, she asked lightly, 'Never want your own family? Or never like that with anyone else's child?'

'You know the answer to both those questions. Or I thought you did.'

She nodded. 'I suppose I do. Lack of sleep catching up.'

'I saw the crossword on the kitchen bench when I got in. How many hours did you get last night?' The concern had returned, but this time annoyance was in the mix.

And she owed him an apology. 'Actually, I did sleep quite well for me, and the crossword was breakfast entertainment.' Not saying she'd started it at three in the morning. 'Now, I'd better get cracking. It's busy in here.' She nudged past him, striding down the hall to the room she was needed in.

'For the record, in case you've forgotten, I do want children of my own with a woman whom I love, and no, I don't get all possessive over someone else's baby.' Raphael was right beside her, his mouth grim. This conversation wasn't over. It was going to be a barrel of laughs at home tonight.

Maybe she'd go to visit Carly. Except she and Adem weren't going to be home tonight. Something about having a meal with family members. All part of the wedding build-up. Lucky girl. Isabella took a sideways look at the man who had her heart in a flutter. What was it like to be planning a wedding with the man of your dreams? Not once had the small celebration she and Darren had turned her heart into an out of control bongo drum. The planning had taken a few hours on the phone, and the dress had been in a sale in the local shop.

Damn it, Isabella, why did you not see how wrong that was at the time?

Because she'd been so desperate to have the life she'd been promised she hadn't seen past the hype. And if she had? Would she be feeling differently about Raphael now? No answer dropped into her head, nothing stopped the tailspin she was in.

Raphael tapped her on the shoulder. 'I'll wait and give you a lift when you're done.'

'That's not necessary.'

'Maybe, but I'll wait anyway.'

CHAPTER SEVEN

'RAPHAEL, CAN YOU take a look at Janice Crowe?' Jacki asked as he left his patient's room. 'Baby's breeched.'

There went any chance of snatching a coffee. 'Room?'

'Three. Janice is eighteen, hasn't been to antenatal classes or seen a doctor for three months.'

So she'd be terrified and blaming everyone else. Raphael sighed. Young women without family support always had a hard time of their pregnancies. 'Bloods?'

'Haemoglobin eighty-six, MCV and MCH indicate iron deficiency. Still waiting for the results on the blood group, iron and liver functions.'

He raised his eyebrow. 'Drugs?'

Jacki shook her head. 'There's a distinct yellow tinge to her skin and eyes.'

Inside room three Isabella was trying to calm the distraught girl. 'Janice, breathe deep. That's it. Keep at it, and you'll help baby.' She glanced up and relief flooded her face when she saw him. 'Here's Mr Dubois, the obstetrician. He's going to help you and baby.'

'Hello, Janice. Call me Raphael,' he said in an attempt to put her at ease. He had her notes in his hand but didn't look at them, instead kept eye contact with his patient. 'I hear your baby's turned the wrong way round.'

Janice nodded, her teeth biting deep into her bottom lip.

Izzy held her hand.

'I have to examine you. Is that all right?' It'd be a problem if she refused as there weren't any female doctors on duty today. 'Or would you prefer Isabella does it? Though I do like to see what's going on myself.'

Janice's mouth flattened, and she stared at him.

He held his breath as he waited for her approval. It went better when the patient was on the same page. This baby was going to be all right. It had to be.

'Okay.'

'Good.' Slipping gloves on, he watched as Izzy talked Janice into lying back and bending her legs, placing her feet apart.

'Now, I am going to lift the sheet up to your waist. At least the room is nice and warm.' She was good with the terrified girl. 'Hold on. That's another contraction, right?' Izzy immediately went to hold Janice's hands until it passed. 'Breathe. You're doing great. That's it.'

Tears spilled down Janice's face. 'It hurts so much.'

'Yes, but the painkiller should be working by now. You need to relax.' Izzy smiled. 'I know. Stupid thing to say, right? But believe me, if you can relax a bit the pain drug will work better. Now, lie back and let Raphael see what baby's up to.'

Raphael positioned himself for the examination. 'Do you know if you're having a boy or girl, Janice?' Chances were she hadn't had a scan, but keeping her talking would make what he was about to do go easier.

'No. When I had my scan it was too early to find out. I want a boy though.'

'Why a boy?' Isabella kept the conversation going, while ready to pass him anything he might require.

Janice shrugged. 'They seem easier.'

Raphael laughed. 'You think? My mother wouldn't agree with you.' His hand felt the baby. Definitely breech, and there was the umbilical cord below the presenting part of baby. His laugh snapped off. They had a problem. This had become urgent. Drawing a breath, he prepared to tell his patient what the next move was. 'Janice, baby is trying to come out feet first and that doesn't work. There's also a complication with the cord being flattened by baby so not enough blood is getting through. Do you understand?'

'I think so. Is my baby going to die?'

'No. I am going to do a C-section. Urgently.'

'You're going to cut it out?'

That was putting it bluntly. 'Yes, I am. It's best for baby, and for you. It doesn't take very long, and means no more contractions. You'll be sore for some days afterwards and need help with baby, but someone will talk to you about that later.'

Izzy pulled down the sheet to cover Janice. 'You're being very brave.'

'Can you stay with me when he takes the baby out?'

Izzy looked at Raphael, one perfectly shaped eyebrow lifted.

'As long as Jacki doesn't mind losing you for a while, it's fine with me.' He had to have a nurse there anyway, and why not Izzy? He liked working with her. 'Right, I'll get the ball rolling.'

'I'll get Janice ready.' Her smile warmed him right to his toes.

There were no hiccups with the C-section. The baby girl was healthy and Janice seemed to have forgotten she wanted a boy as she gazed down at her precious bundle.

Raphael felt the tension between his shoulder blades back off as he accepted that another baby had made its way into the world and was going to be all right. There were a lot of hurdles ahead for Janice and her daughter, but he'd done his bit for them and got it right.

He and Izzy. He watched as she tended to Janice, getting her a drink of water, wiping her face, constantly keeping an eye on the baby, showing Janice how to hold her, to rub her. Oh, yes, Izzy was good at this.

His mouth dried and his heart thumped. What was he going to do?

Just after midnight on Wednesday Isabella lifted the ward phone and speed-dialled Raphael. 'You're needed. Tania Newman's showing signs of puerperal sepsis.'

'I'm putting you on speaker phone so you can fill me in on the details while I dress.'

That she did not need to think about. 'Heart and resp rates are high, BP's down, and she's running a temperature. White count an hour ago was slightly elevated but no indicators of infection.'

'Any abdo pain that's nothing to do with contractions?'

'Yes, and she's started vomiting.'

'I'm heading out the door now. Take another blood for CBC, mark it urgent,' Raphael told her. 'Always happens at night time, doesn't it?' Click. He was gone.

Had he really had time to haul on some pants and a shirt? Guess he was used to dressing in seconds. There was always a pile of clothes on his dresser, no doubt just for moments like this. Isabella rushed back to Tania's room with the phlebotomy kit in her hand. 'Mr Dubois's on his way. He wants another blood test done.'

Katie, the nurse on with her, nodded. 'You take the sample while I wipe Tania down again.'

Isabella set the kit on the bed beside the terrified woman. 'Tania, I know you don't like needles but this is really important.'

'Do whatever you have to,' the thirty-four-year-old woman grunted through her pain. 'Just save my baby.'

'We're doing everything we can, and like I said, Raphael is on his way. Pushing his speed to the limit, I bet.'

'Hope he's careful. We need him here,' Dominic Newman said as he held his wife's hand, looking lost and nothing like the notorious criminal lawyer he was. Babies were great levellers. 'What can I do? There's got to be something other than sitting here like a useless lump.'

'You're on keeping Tania calm duty.' It was a big ask. The woman was frantic with worry and fear.

'I read about puerperal sepsis on a website,' Tania cried. 'It's bad. Really bad. Baby might not make it.'

True, sepsis at this stage of pregnancy was not good. 'Sometimes I wish the internet had never been invented.' Isabella slid the tourniquet up Tania's arm. 'Tighten your hand into a fist. That's it. Now, a small prick.' She hit the vein immediately and released the tourniquet as the tube filled.

'Why do you always say that? It's not the first time I've had my blood taken,' Tania shouted.

'It's routine.' Isabella drew the blood, placed a cotton ball over the site and slid the needle out. 'There you go. All done.' She named the tube and filled out a form, marked it urgent. 'I'll get that up to the lab now. Hopefully we'll have the results by the time Mr Dubois gets here.' Hopefully the lab tech would make a film when he received the sample and not wait to find out what the white count was. The film would be required to do a white cell differential count to ascertain the number of neutrophil band forms which were indicative of infection. The more bands and even earlier forms of that particular white cell, the stronger the infection.

'Agh!' Tania cried, and straightened out on the bed, grabbing at Dominic and gripping his wrists like a vice.

His face paled, but he didn't budge, let his wife squeeze as though her life depended on it.

'Deep breaths,' Isabella said, and rubbed her shoulder constantly until the spasm passed. 'Well done.'

'Like I had any choice,' Tania snapped.

'Hey, steady, darling. Isabella and Katie are here to help us.'

'It's all right.' Katie grinned. 'We've heard worse.'

'I'm sorry.' Tania looked contrite. 'I really

am. It's just so painful, and then this puerperal infection. I'm terrified.' She struggled upright and leaned her head in against Dominic, who took over the rubbing.

'Can I take a look at your cervix?' Isabella preferred asking rather than just saying that's what she had to do. A simple question gave her patient some sense of control over a situation where she had absolutely none. Especially in this case. As soon as Raphael got here there'd be a lot going on, and Tania wouldn't be given a chance to say anything. Urgency was now a major factor in this delivery. If this was PS, then the infection would run away on them if they weren't careful. Antibiotics had already been administered, but Rafe might up the dosage.

'Why have I got an infection down there?'

Katie answered, 'You said your breasts were sore when you first arrived, and I thought it looked as though you've got a small infection in your nipples.'

'The other doctor gave me antibiotics for it. She said it would be all right for baby to take them.'

'The infection could've already spread, and the symptoms have only just begun showing up in the last little while.'

Isabella waited until Tania gulped hard and nodded at her. 'Go for it. Hopefully baby's nearly here and we can get this nightmare over and done with. What if he gets the infection too?'

That was the problem. 'Mr Dubois will explain everything when he arrives.' Ducking for cover, but it wasn't her place to fill this couple in on what might happen. Times like this she was glad to be a nurse and midwife, and not a doctor. They could have handing out the grim news. She'd seen how much it upset Raphael. Tugging on gloves she positioned herself at the end of the bed and waited for Tania to lie back. 'Okay, try and relax.'

It didn't take long to get the measurement and Isabella felt relief. 'Nine centimetres. We're nearly there.'

'About time,' Tania grumped. 'I've had enough.'

There was still the pushing to undertake, but best keep that to herself for now. No point in upsetting her patient any more than she already was. Hopefully Raphael would be here before they started.

'Hello, Tania, Dominic.' The man himself strode into the room minutes later, looking beyond calm.

But Isabella knew better, saw the tell-tale sign where his mouth tightened in one corner. 'That was quick.'

'The roads were fairly quiet for a change. Right, let's see what's happening, shall we? Tania, tell me about the pain in your belly.'

From then on everything happened fast. A phone call came from the lab alerting them to the CBC results and the raised white cell and band form counts. Raphael administered another antibiotic intravenously. Tania began pushing before she was told to, and reluctantly stopped, only to have baby make her own mind up that it was time to come, and soon it was over. Baby Sophie met her parents, had a brief, safe cuddle from each before being whisked into the specialised cot and wiped over extra carefully because of the infection mum had.

'I'm going to give Sophie antibiotics too,' Raphael told the worried parents. 'We don't know yet if she'd caught the infection, but I prefer to be on the safe side. You have to understand what this means.' He ran through what could go wrong, then reassured them it was unlikely, but they had to know. 'Then she'll go to PICU where they'll monitor her continuously.'

Tania was crying. 'I want to hold her. I want her here, not on a different floor.' She hiccupped. 'I know what you're doing is the right thing, but it's so unfair. We've waited years for her and now we can't keep her with us.'

Dominic wrapped his wife in his arms, tears streaming down his face to mingle with hers. 'Shh, darling. It's going to be all right.'

Raphael talked to the couple some more, working at pacifying them.

When he'd finished, Isabella looked at him and Katie, and they nodded agreement, then left the room quietly, pushing Sophie's cot ahead of them.

'Phew,' Isabella sighed. 'It never gets any easier with distraught parents.'

'The day it does is the time for you to walk out of here and go work as an interior decorator.' Raphael chuckled. 'Me, I'll learn to play the banjo and sit on my back step all day.'

Katie agreed. 'I'll find a rich man and retire for good. Right, come on, Sophie, let's get you settled in PICU.'

As Katie headed down the corridor at a fast clip with her special cargo, Isabella's heart went with the wee tot. 'She's so vulnerable.'

Raphael moved closer. '*Oui*, they all are. I wonder how something so fragile and tiny can be so strong. It scares me sometimes.'

'Would we be worse parents because we know all the things that can go wrong?'

'I'd say so. I've seen it often enough with colleagues who've had babies on my watch. Their pregnancies are hard work.' He didn't blink at her use of 'we'.

But then she hadn't meant it as in we, us, together. Had she? Oh, hell. Get busy, find someone who needed her attention. Raphael would go home soon. Fingers crossed.

But now he looked worried. 'Who can tell with these things? Right, I'd better go inter-

rupt the couple and do some more checks on
Tania before I head away.'

'Hopefully you'll get home before it's time
to get up and come to work.' She still had five
hours to get through before knocking off at
seven. By the time she reached home Raphael
would be back here. Ships in the night. It
should be ideal. No talking about things that
got her in a knot, or brought that faraway look
to his eyes when he was watching her. No
wishing she could sit down and tell him the
truth. To say out loud that she wanted more
from their relationship but was afraid to act
on it for fear of hurting both of them, especially Rafe. To explain she could not give him
what he deserved after how Cassie treated
him, and still she wanted to try.

'I'll do my best.' He shrugged. 'You got
anything planned for the day once you've had
some sleep?'

'A second inspection of the apartment I'm
renting.'

His face dropped. Had he not believed
she'd move out? She'd thought he'd be only

too happy when that day came. Seemed it wasn't only her who was all over the place in what they wanted.

Friday and the end of a particularly drama-filled week with patients. Raphael felt his body come alive at the thought of a free week-end ahead. What would he do with it? Spend time with Izzy when she wasn't working? Go and see where she was intending to move to. Visit the shops. There was quite a bit of shopping for kitchenware and furniture going on at the moment, and the landing on his second floor was filling up with packages and small cartons. Every time he walked past to his bedroom his heart slowed. She was definitely setting up her own home. Getting on with her life. He could learn from her. Find the courage to do the same.

Raphael let himself into the house and stopped. Paint fumes hit him. A foreign lightness in the hall made him gape. Wow. What a difference. Should've done it years ago. Except there'd been no motivation before. Izzy had changed everything.

She stood at the bottom of the stairs, dressed in over-large paint-spattered overalls with a roller in one hand and a wide grin on her face. A paint smear streaked across her cheek. Cute. Sexy. 'What do you think?'

I think I want to kiss that spot.

His stomach crunched, his blood hummed.

I think I want to kiss your soft lips and taste you.

Forget humming. There was a torrent in his veins. He was over waiting, being patient, giving her time. He had to do something about his feelings for her.

Dragging his eyes away from the sight that had him in meltdown, he looked around at the white with a hint of grey walls, woodwork, ceiling, and felt his mouth lifting into a smile that grew and grew. 'Amazing. Who'd have believed getting rid of that magenta could make such a difference. This hall is twice the size it was when I went to work this morning.'

'That's a relief.' She placed the roller in the clean tray.

'You were worried I wouldn't like it?' He stepped closer, put his keys and phone on the bottom stair and stood there watching the varying emotions flitting through her beautiful old-wood-coloured eyes.

'Not really.' Her teeth nibbling her lip told him otherwise.

He had to force himself not to reach over and place a finger on her lips to stop her action. 'Why wouldn't I? It was me who bought the paint two years ago.'

Izzy shifted her weight from one foot to the other, then lifted her head enough to lock those eyes on his. 'I worried I've overstepped the mark by doing this without telling you what I was up to.'

Izzy never worried about upsetting him. Carrying on with whatever *she* thought best was a trademark of their friendship, always had been, and was one of the reasons he adored her. Something was off centre here, and it frustrated him not knowing what that was. 'Relax. I'm more than happy with what you've done. In fact, I'm blown away.' He waved a hand at his new hall. 'This is amazing. It fires me up to get on with doing up the rest of the house.'

He hadn't noticed the tension in her shoulders until they softened, and a smile touched those lips. 'Thank you, Isabella.'

Her eyes widened and she glanced away, came back to lock eyes with him again. The tip of her tongue appeared at the corner of her mouth. 'Phew.'

Raphael could not stop himself. He reached out, placed his hands on her arms and drew her closer. 'Again, thanks. By doing this you've starting turning my house into a home and up until now I hadn't realised how important it is if I'm to continue living here and become ensconced in a London lifestyle, not just working at the hospital every available hour.'

She was shaking under his hands.

His thumbs smoothed circles on her arms. 'Izzy.'

Her breasts rose, stilled, dropped again. 'Rafe.'

Afterwards he didn't remember moving, couldn't recall anything but his mouth on hers at last. Soft. Sweet. Isabella. Strong, tough Izzy. Returning his kiss. Returning his kiss!

She tasted of promise, of fun and love, of life. And then her tongue nudged past his into his mouth and the world stood still. While his body fizzed, the thudding behind his ribs frantic, his groin tightening, and tightening further. It felt like an out-of-body experience, yet his feet were firmly planted on the stair below her. His hands were holding Izzy's arms, now sliding around to bring her in close, closer, up against his body, chest to breast, her thighs against his groin, mouth to mouth. Kiss for kiss.

Yes. This was what he'd been waiting for. Izzy. She'd always been there, in his blood, his heart, but not like this. Until that day she married someone else and he woke up.

She moved, slid her mouth away, leaned back to stare up at him.

She'd better not have read his mind right then.

Her tongue was licking her bottom lip. Tasting him? Her throat bobbed. Her eyes were saucers, big, golden globes of heat and desire. 'Oh, Rafe,' she whispered through what sounded like need—for him.

His own need was pulsing throughout his body. 'Izzy? You all right? With this?' *Please, please, please say yes.*

A slow nod.

'I...' He hesitated. Talk too much and kill the moment. Don't explain where he was coming from and risk having her change her mind, and running for the hills. 'I want to be more than friends. Have for a long time now.'

Another nod. This time with a hint of concern darkening that golden gaze.

'You don't agree? I should stick to being friends?'

Raphael wants me.

Isabella wanted to let go her grip on his shoulders, to step back, take time to think this through. But if she removed her hands, couldn't feel him under her palms, she'd curl up and die. She wanted him. Yes, she was admitting it at last. She wanted Rafe. But that fear was still there, lurking at the edges of her mind. What if she failed him? What if it didn't work out? She'd lose the most important person in her life.

He was waiting. Patiently. Yet there was tension in his muscles. She felt it under her hands, saw it in his jaw, knew it in his eyes. Had he thought beyond this moment? Of course he would've. This was Raphael—not Mr Spontaneity, not Mr Take-What-I-Can-Get-and-to-Hell-with-the-Consequences. Friends or lovers? She could not continue being neutral. Had to stop playing safe. Digging deep, she found it wasn't so hard to ask, 'Want to go upstairs?'

He lifted her off the stairs, held her against him. 'Thought you'd never ask.'

Slipping her arms around his neck she gazed at this man she'd always known and was now going to learn about in an entirely different way, and let go all the hang-ups, the questions, the need to be someone, and went with being who she was, who she had. Raphael. Nuzzling his neck, she smiled when his arms tightened around her as he carried her up to his bedroom.

He lay her on the bed.

Oh, no, you don't.

She leapt up, stood in front of him and

reached for the first button on his shirt, slowly slid it through the buttonhole and leaned close to kiss the spot she'd revealed. Then the next button, and licked his skin, smiling when he groaned. The third button, and Rafe's hands skimmed down her back to clasp her butt.

The fourth button and her head was spinning with need.

Those strong hands were lifting her up against his erection. His manhood pressing into her belly. OMG.

The fifth and— She had to stop or this would be over before it got any further. She couldn't stop. Her whole body was crying out for release, yet she wanted so much more, wanted to touch all of him, every inch of skin. Forget the buttons. She jerked the shirt out of his waistband and pushed it up.

Rafe lifted his head enough for her to tug the annoying shirt off. Then she went back to kissing and licking that smooth skin, and absorbing the hits of sharp desire stabbing her belly, her breasts, her centre. Hands on her waist, then she was wobbling on her feet as the domes of the overalls were pulled open.

The oversized boiler suit fell to her hips, then to the floor, unaided by Rafe's hands now intent on lifting her T-shirt and touching her— everywhere.

A groan slid across her swollen lips as his thumbs rubbed her nipples, arousing them further, tightening them into painful knobs of pulsing need. Her own hands were claws against Raphael, trying to caress while tightening further as the need in her deepened to the point she lost all comprehension of what was happening. 'Rafe. Please,' she begged. 'I can't take any more.'

Her bra hit the floor, her panties slid down to her ankles with the help of one of those hot hands. He quickly grabbed a small packet from the drawer beside the bed, tore the packet open and rolled the condom on. Then he was lifting her to his waist, turning around to lean her against the wall as she wound her legs around him. 'Izzy,' he growled.

His hot tip touched her centre.

She tried to reach for him, to hold him intimately.

Another throaty growl. 'Not yet. Won't last.' And he was filling her, giving to her.

Her head tipped back against the wall and she rocked with the need exploding throughout her body. 'Rafe,' she screamed.

Then with a guttural roar he took her, his body tense as he came.

They lay on his bed, legs and arms tangled, lungs working hard, eyes closed.

Wow. Isabella sighed. Never would've thought she could feel like this. As if she'd found something so special it might break if she wasn't careful.

'Don't go there, Isabella.'

See? He knew her too well. Rolling onto her tummy and sprawling half across him she eyeballed him. 'It's hard not to.'

He winced.

Immediately she lifted up to kiss him. 'I am not sorry.' Kiss. 'I'm mind-blown.' There was no comparison between her feelings for Raphael and those she'd believed she had for Darren.

A return kiss that lasted longer than hers to

him, and started clouding the subject. 'That's two of us.'

There was so much she wanted to tell him. How she loved him, wanted to always be with him. But what if she did let him down? That was too awful to contemplate. She still didn't know if she'd got it right. Look what happened last time she told a man she loved him. Not that she was ready to utter the L word. Afraid to, more likely. Rolling onto her back as he got up to dispose of the condom in his bathroom, she stared up at the ceiling that was desperately in need of a coat of paint. 'Pinch me.'

He came back into the bedroom and lay back down next to her. 'Please don't say you're already regretting this.'

Reaching for his hand, she held on tight. 'Not at all. Why would I?' Hell, what if Rafe only wanted sex, and had no wish for a future with her? Hadn't thought of that, had she?

Raphael rose onto his elbow and gazed down at her. If she didn't know better she'd say that was love coming her way. But it couldn't be. Not the 'this is for ever, sexy, everything together' kind of love.

When he remained quiet, she had to ask, 'What?' Her heart smashed against her ribs as she waited for him to reply.

At last, 'Nothing.' That was it? Then he kissed her and her muscles loosened a little.

Wrapping her arms around his strong, muscular body, she pulled him into her. She'd hopped off the fence on the side of go for it, and was ready to give this everything she had. But not ready to talk about it. That might ruin everything.

Raphael gathered her into his arms and began making love to her like he had no intention of ever stopping. She could live with this for as long as it was on offer. Reality would step in some time, but for now she was safe from the demons that liked to wreak havoc with her dreams.

Raphael yawned. It was his turn not to sleep. How could he with Izzy wrapped around him like a limpet? A warm, soft one. Okay, not a limpet, but the best damned thing to have happened to him in a long time, if not in for ever.

Sensationnelle.

He'd poured years of emotions into his lovemaking during the night. Had he always loved her?

But if that were true, then he wouldn't have been so devastated by what Cassie had done to him.

He shivered. Slow down. Think it through. Last night had been amazing, but it didn't change anything. He and Izzy were still friends, and despite being intimate, that hadn't changed. Other than to put pressure on him to get it right. Big pressure. Izzy was vulnerable, still coming to terms with Darren's treachery. She didn't need him trying to get too close, too fast, and then finding he wasn't ready to commit to her either. Because he was still struggling to accept the loss of his child, and why. Especially the why. If he told Izzy about Joshua it might free some of the knots holding him back, but he didn't want her to see his vulnerability. That was saying he wasn't as tough as she believed him to be.

His body tightened, and not in the way it had often during the night as they made love. He had to tell her. It would be a lie not to. She was entitled to know everything, otherwise he would never be able ask her to become a part of his life when he was ready. If he was ever ready. *Thump, thump* went his heavy heart.

'Rafe?' Izzy muttered.

'Oui, mon amie?' Stick to friend, keep this real.

Her reply was a small snore.

So, not ready to talk. Thank goodness. He could continue the dream by lying here, holding her warm, sexy body against him, feeling her hot breaths on his skin, knowing she was relaxed with him as she hadn't been since she arrived. But this was Isabella. There'd be questions and concerns scooting round her mind about whether they were doing the right thing, how long this could last, was it for ever or a rerun of her marriage. Knowing her meant he was forewarned.

And this *was* Izzy. He couldn't hurt her in any way. He had to back off until he sorted out his mess. Had to. No other way to go forward. But how, now that he knew Izzy intimately?

How, when she was living in his house for another few weeks?

When he was going to the wedding with her?

Damn, he'd made the situation between them worse, not better.

CHAPTER EIGHT

OUT ON THE DECK, Isabella stretched onto her toes, leaned back to ease the rest of the kinks out of her muscles that a long soak under a hot shower hadn't fixed. What a night. What a lover Rafe had turned out to be. She'd never known sex to be so wonderful.

And then she'd slept like she hadn't in for ever. Right through to ten in the morning. Why? She'd have thought the excitement of making love with Raphael would've kept her awake all night, not knocked her out. Had she found her safe place with Rafe? No, couldn't have. Must've been because he'd exhausted her with his lovemaking. But she did feel different. Relaxed and happy.

Why wasn't he here? It had stung a little to wake up and find herself alone in his bed. He hadn't been downstairs when she made her way to the kitchen. There'd been a note saying he'd gone for a run and might go into work afterwards. As though putting distance between them. Was he regretting last night already?

Her heart sank. He wouldn't. He might.

Then what? She'd have to suck it up and get on with her plans of setting up the flat she was about to rent. She had to do that anyway. Just because they'd become lovers didn't mean she would change everything. She still had to make her own life work for her. Preferably including Raphael. But she was not going to follow him or anyone to do what they wanted without keeping herself true to herself. She'd messed up once. It wasn't happening again, if she could help it.

Her phone rang.

Rafe.

She snatched it up. 'Hey, good morning. Where are you? I didn't wake up for hours. I feel so good.' Shut up, let the man say why he rang.

'Could've set a bomb off and you wouldn't

have woken. Guess I've got my uses, then.' He laughed.

'Seems like it.'

'Feel like going to the movies and dinner tonight?'

Pardon? 'As in a date?'

Silence. Then, 'Yes, a date.'

He could sound more enthusiastic. 'You sure that's what you want to do? I mean, if last night was a one-night stand say so.' Get the pain over with now.

'Yes, Isabella, I do want to take you out. And…'

She gritted her teeth. 'Go on.' He was about to break her heart.

'I don't want it to be a one-night stand.'

Phew.

Then, 'But I admit I'm uncertain where we're going with this.'

How about into a relationship that would blossom into love? 'We don't have to rush it, Rafe.' Her heart was squeezing painfully. 'I've got things to think about too.'

'I know. That's also what's holding me back. So, you still want to go out tonight?'

Did she? 'Yes, I do.' She could be setting herself up for a fall, but sometimes she had to take a chance.

'See you about six, then.' And he was gone.

She stared at her phone. Did that just happen? He hadn't said where he was. It was the weekend and he wasn't rostered on the ward but bet that's where he was. It was his bolt hole, she realised. Put a bed in a corner, and fill a cupboard with his clothes and he'd never come home. No wonder he hadn't got around to redecorating.

Chienne rubbed against her leg.

'Hey, you. At least I know where I'm at with you.' She lifted the cat onto her shoulder for a cuddle. 'I've got a date with your dad.'

A date meant dressing up in something decent. And if she wanted a repeat of last night whatever she chose to wear had better be more interesting than jeans and a shirt.

Raphael stared at the apparition in red standing in his lounge. *Sacré bleu.* This was Izzy? He could feel his heart exploding against his ribs, while his groin was tightening. 'I want to rush upstairs and tear that dress off you.' It had to be the sexiest dress he'd ever seen, and yet he wanted to remove it?

'That bad, huh?' She grinned.

'Oh, yes.' This had to stop or they'd never make it to the restaurant and as much as he wanted to make love with Izzy he was taking her on a proper date so they could calm down after last night. Put some perspective on things. Except she'd gone and raised the bar to impossible heights. Somehow he had to be strong, stop being diverted by a red ball of sex on amazing legs and ladder-high shoes. Reaching for her hand, he tugged her close and began walking to the front door, past the stairs that'd take them up to his bedroom. 'Let's get out of here while we're still capable.' Except her hand was soft, small in his, and adding to the need clawing through his body. So much for pulling back.

Hopefully the movie would be scintillating and he'd forget all about his companion. As if.

A couple of hours later Raphael had to admit it hadn't been too bad. He had forgotten Izzy enough for his body to quieten down. 'What did you think?'

'That I prefer romance movies to fantasy.'

'Got that wrong, didn't I?' He looked around. 'Let's give that bar a go. Or do you want to choose since I got the movie wrong?'

'There's good.' She wasn't sounding as excited as she had earlier.

Which might be good since he was trying to slow things down. 'Wine?'

'Please.' She found them a table in the back of the room and shuffled her cute butt onto a stool.

And his body went back to tightening and wanting. While his mind tried to deny everything.

In his pocket his personal phone vibrated. He ignored it. He shouldn't have brought it with him, but who knew when it might be needed in an emergency. For the first time in ages his hospital call phone was on the table at home since he wasn't on call. There were other specialists to cover his patients if the need arose. No one was interrupting them tonight.

'How is Grand'mère?' Izzy asked. 'Back on her bike yet?'

'Not quite. Or she's not admitting it if she is. I'd have to tell her off.'

'Yes, and she'd laugh at you, so no problem.'

'She rang today. She wants me to go home for a visit sometime soon.' He paused.

Izzy sipped her drink, her gaze fixed on him over the rim of the glass. 'To spend time with her? Or is there something else happening?'

Was this Izzy's way of asking did he still intend moving home one day? 'Only that she wants to catch up and it's easier for me to make the trip at the moment. She suggested you tag along too.'

'I'd love to.' Izzy was still watching him like she was looking for something more. Of course she was. She'd be thinking that if he was over Cassie enough to have a fling with her, then he could very well be ready enough to move back to France. She might be right, and how would she feel about that? Her growing excitement and determination to make

London home would come down in a rush, sending her back to wondering if she could ever settle anywhere and be happy. She could relax on that score. He wasn't going to wreck her newfound happiness, even if that meant ruining his own before he got started.

Raphael gazed at Isabella, his mind stumped with the way he'd been blindsided with their lovemaking. He'd felt as though he'd found something he'd been looking for all his life. Yet it scared the pants off him. He wasn't ready. Might never be. But to walk away without trying might be beyond him. It might be too soon for Isabella as well. Not to mention the Joshua hurdle for him to get over. He'd never thought it would be so hard to tell Izzy. Sure, no one else knew either, but this was so much more important. It scared him to reveal the depth of his pain and anger. Holding on to those emotions was the one grip on keeping himself complete he had. Airing it might undo him so much that he'd never be the same again.

'Earth to Raphael.' Her warm hand covered his. 'Where have you gone?'

Quick, come up with something. 'Thinking about when we can manage to go over to Avignon together.' Together? He really wasn't keeping back from this, was he?

'We'll have to pick a weekend we're both off.'

'Of course.'

Their pizzas arrived, looking and smelling delicious. And tasting just as good.

Izzy asked, 'I know Grand'mère says she's getting out and about as though the hip operation never happened, but do you think she might've slowed down? Might be starting to think about the future in a different light?'

'I do. She says she's not ready to move out of the family home, and is thrilled Maman and Papa have moved in. As soon as she's getting around properly she'll take the downstairs rooms and save herself those horrendous stairs now that she's had a fall.'

'Bet she already thinks she's capable,' Izzy said, those golden eyes focused entirely on him. 'It's your family tradition for someone from each generation to live in the family house at some stage, isn't it?'

'*Oui.* Though my parents have taken a while to get there.'

'You haven't thought of skipping a generation and moving in yourself?'

Damn. Should've kept his mouth shut. 'Izzy.' He reached for her hand. 'I live here. I'm still not ready to return to Avignon.' *Please believe me.* Why should she when he didn't?

Tipping her head to one side, she studied him so intently she must've been able to see everything he was striving to keep to himself. As bumps lifted on his skin, she said, 'As long as you're sure. And happy.' Then she picked up a slab of pizza and ate so calmly that he struggled to believe she'd been any different moments ago.

If Isabella remained determined to make London home, then he might have to factor that into any decisions he made about his future. His heart slowed. He did want to return home one day. He also wanted to have Izzy in his future once he'd laid everything else to rest.

As soon as the pizza was finished, Izzy

pushed her plate away and stood up. 'I'm ready to go home.' The gold returned to her brown eyes. 'I'm whacked.'

'You and me both.' Physically and mentally.

Isabella could feel her heart pounding on the quiet drive home. She couldn't make Rafe out. He was on edge, like he didn't want to be with her while at the same time he enjoyed her company.

What had changed since last night? Had he got cold feet? Raphael, Mr Confident, running scared? Couldn't be. Was he going to let her down too? Hardly. He hadn't made any promises about anything. Could be it had been a one-night fling. Except she couldn't accept that. They were too close for that. Or was that the problem? They were close and he was afraid they'd lose it all? *That* she could understand.

Pulling into the drive, he said, 'Thanks for the night. I enjoyed it.'

That was it?

'Me too.'

She shoved the door open and clambered

out in an ungainly fashion with her high heels. So not used to wearing anything so far off the ground. Making her way inside she waited by the front door until Raphael joined her.

'I might do some work on the computer,' he muttered, looking everywhere but at her.

Isabella placed her arms around his neck and leaned in against him, tipping back enough to look into his startled face. 'You really want to do that?'

'I think it's best.'

For who? She stretched up on her toes and placed her lips on his mouth.

His hands took her hips. To pull her forward? Or push her away?

She pressed her mouth over his, slid her tongue inside. Tasted him. Slipped out and back in.

'Izzy,' he groaned. 'Stop.' His hands tightened their hold of her, tugged gently so her stomach touched his need.

And he wanted her to stop? Try again, Rafe.

Now he was kissing her, possessing her, giving as much as she was offering him.

Pressing her peaked nipples against his chest sent ripples of desire racing through her, heating her body, fizzing her blood.

'Isabella.' Strong hands lifted her away, put space between them.

Isabella.

He was serious. 'Don't you dare say we can't do this. Not now,' she growled.

Not when I'm pulsing with need for you.

'You don't understand.'

'Damn right, I don't.'

'I can't promise you anything, Izzy.'

She relaxed at Izzy. 'I haven't asked you to.'

'I know.' He was still holding her. 'I might hurt you.'

True, and she might hurt him. 'I'm a big girl, Rafe. I'll take whatever happens on the chin.'

'Yes, but…'

She placed a finger over his mouth. 'But nothing, Raphael. Make love to me. Please.'

Those dark eyes locked on her, searching for what she had no idea. There was apprehension in his gaze, which was slowly replaced by excitement. 'If you're sure,' he said as he swung her up into his arms and carried her upstairs.

Very sure. If there were consequences, then she'd manage. It would hurt but she could not walk away from tonight.

Isabella looked through the window to the beautiful garden beyond where Carly and Adem's wedding ceremony would take place in a few minutes. She was so happy for her friend. She also couldn't help wondering if she and Raphael would ever get to this point. They'd had an amazing week, making love every night, but there was an obvious hesitation in his approach to her, as though he wasn't ready. Which he had kind of intimated on their date night. Well, she wasn't one hundred per cent ready either but she was up to giving it a chance by working hard to keep the doubt gremlins quiet, and believing in herself. The past was over, the doubts brought about by Darren finished with. But she wasn't here to think about that. This was Carly's day.

'Isn't this a gorgeous setting?' she said to Esther. The gardens were colourful with roses and peonies and other flowers bright in the sunshine.

'Magic. And don't we all look swish in our silk dresses?'

'Not bad at all.' Raphael was standing with her friends' men, looking completely at ease. The moment Carly knew he was accompanying her to the wedding, he'd been told he'd be Isabella's escort when they stood with Carly and Adem as they exchanged their vows. What was he thinking? Would he ever want to get married again?

'Lily, no.' Esther grabbed Lily's hand before Carly's bouquet of blue flowers was destroyed. 'Come on. We'd better get this show happening before little miss here does something we'll all regret.'

'Group hug first,' Carly said as she approached them. She looked beautiful in her dress with her hair falling free over her shoulders, and a small baby bump beginning to show.

Tears threatened to spurt down Isabella's face. 'You look stunning. And so happy.'

The four women gathered close to hug,

tears on everyone's faces. 'So much for the make-up,' Chloe laughed.

'Me.' Lily pulled at her mother's skirt. 'I want a hug.'

She got four, then Isabella, Chloe and Esther gathered around Carly to lead her out to the garden to get married.

The ceremony was short, spoke of love and commitment and had every female in the garden in tears. Glancing sideways at Raphael, panic struck. Here was a man she truly loved, with everything she had. Yet she couldn't celebrate. He wasn't showing signs of loving her back. What if she was doomed to another broken heart? This time would be far harder to get over than her previous mistake. Swallowing hard, she dragged in air to calm the banging in her chest. She could not get upset or worried today. Not when her girlfriend was celebrating finding the love of her life, and *she* was standing beside Raphael.

'Knew I'd need this.' Rafe handed her a handkerchief. 'Brand new, just for you.' His smile was soppy, like he too was feeling the love going on. And why wouldn't he be?

There wasn't a soul in the garden who didn't look the same.

'Ta,' she sniffed, dabbing her nose and eyes, and doing her best not to mess up her make-up. Mascara under the eyes was such a great look. Except by the time Carly and Adem slid rings onto each other's fingers the make-up was long gone, and Raphael had passed her a second handkerchief, pocketing the first one, sodden and stained blue-black. When Adem leaned in to kiss Carly, Isabella clapped, hiding the sudden spike of jealousy.

'You're such a softie.' Rafe grinned, then blinked, looking away.

'And you're not?'

'Un peu.'

'Sure.'

A little? Underneath that serious specialist façade was an emotional man who was good at hiding his feelings when he felt they'd be used against him. She gave a little gasp. Was that the cause of his hesitation to talk about the future? He had something to hide?

Not now, Isabella.

True. She was wasting a wonderful occasion worrying about herself. Today wasn't about her. Or Raphael. 'Weddings do that some people.'

'Not me usually. But for some reason today feels extra special.' He was looking into her eyes, right in, while smiling that sensitive, loving smile she adored.

What was he saying? 'It is.' She gave him back a smile. One that told him the words she hadn't managed to utter yet. *I love you.* 'There are weddings, and then there are other weddings. This is one of the best kind.'

Raphael's lips brushed her brow. 'You look beautiful, Izzy. Inside and out.'

'How many handkerchiefs did you bring?' she asked around a lump in her throat. Gone was her ability to fob off words she didn't know how to deal with by saying something witty or growly.

'It was a three-pack.' He stepped back and looked around the garden, suddenly very interested in the roses.

Great. She'd gone and lost him again. He was doing that more and more. She loved it when he kissed her. He made her feel cherished and at ease with her life. Yet all the time those doubts kept surfacing. How long was this going to last? Would they get more involved, or would he walk away? What did he want out of life?

An image of Raphael holding a baby in the maternity ward snapped into her head. Babies. He wanted a family. Still, there was a 'but' hanging around that he hadn't explained. And she still had to conquer her fear of letting him down. Drawing in a breath, she flipped from her worries to her friends. 'Right, I'm going to hug the bride.'

'I'm coming with you.'

Thought he might. 'Carly, I am so happy for you.' Isabella wound her arms around her friend.'

'You're next,' Carly whispered against her.

Her happiness plummeted. Don't say that. Might be tempting fate. 'Oh, that's a long way away off. I'm just enjoying the sex,' she whispered back.

Carly pulled back, stared at her in astonishment. 'You're not certain this will come to anything?'

'Just being cautious, that's all. Now I need to give Adem a hug.' And shut Carly down. She moved sideways to the bridegroom. 'Adem, congratulations. You look beyond happy.'

'I am, Isabella. Way beyond.' He wrapped her up in a hug, then turned to shake Raphael's hand. 'Right, can we get a drink now? Or do I have to abstain all afternoon?'

'Let's go inside. There's cocktails for everyone, and the dinner will also be in there.' Carly was waving to someone else, and when Isabella turned she saw Chloe and Esther coming their way.

'We're heading inside,' she told them.

'Good idea,' Esther said, nodding at the greying sky. 'It's chilled down a little out here, and doesn't look like improving. These dresses are amazing but they're not made for warmth.'

'Off the shoulder leaves a lot of bare skin,' Isabella agreed. Checking that Raphael was still talking to Adem, she saw that Xander and Harry had joined them, and more handshakes and stiff male hugs were going on.

The four men got on very well, which made it easier for her and the other women. Nothing worse than a partner who didn't fit in with your circle of friends. Isabella spied Lily about to step into the garden and went to take her hand and head inside. 'Do you want something yummy to eat?'

'Chocolate?'

'Maybe later. How about some little cheese bickies first?'

'Will I like them?'

'We'll get some and find out.' All the other guests were now inside the understated room that spoke of class, and accepting the glasses of champagne being handed around. Izzy grinned. 'Just like old times.'

'What? Us together?' Chloe nodded. 'It is, isn't it?'

'I'm hungry,' Carly said. 'I was too nervous before the wedding, and the baby needs food.'

Isabella agreed. 'I'll bring one of those of hors-d'oeuvre plates over from the table.'

The day disappeared into evening while they ate dinner and drank toasts, and people made speeches, and had a wonderful time.

Then Adem stood up and placed his hand on his wife's elbow to bring her up beside him. 'Thank you for sharing our special day, everyone. But now, we're going to leave you and head to our hotel.'

Everything wrapped quickly after the newlyweds left.

'Ready to hit the road?' Raphael asked.

'I guess. We're all done here.' Suddenly she didn't want to go back to the house and find out if Rafe was going to make love to her or if tonight was one he said he had work to do. Like he had twice last week. 'Or we could go clubbing.'

He shook his head. 'Not me. I'm more than ready to hit the sack.'

With or without me?

'Fine. Let's go.'

'Isabella, I'm sorry if I've let you down.'

She sighed. 'It's all right. Really. I'm feeling a little deflated after such a wonderful wedding, that's all.'

The ride was so slow and yet sped by. Isabella couldn't wait to get out of the car yet didn't want to stop. She couldn't face being turned down by Raphael heading to his office to work. As if he really had any that needed dealing with tonight. Was this when she stepped up? Put her feelings out there? Let him know she wanted more, not less? Her chest ached with the pounding going on behind her ribs. *Be strong, be brave.*

The moment Raphael shut them in the house she turned to him, reaching her arms up and around his neck.

He tensed. 'Isabella.' Never a good sign when he used her full name.

'You're not working tonight.' Then she stretched up to kiss him, long and hard, and he kissed her back, demanding, giving, sensual.

Yes. She smiled under his mouth, and ran her hands down his back and under his jacket. Tugged his shirt free, touched his skin with her fingertips, absorbed his groans through their kiss. Yes.

Raphael pulled away, stared down at her. 'Izzy.' Better than Isabella.

She put her finger on his mouth. 'Don't say a word.' Then she pushed his jacket down his arms and let it drop to the floor. The shirt was next, and then his belt and fly and his trousers landed around his feet.

Raphael stepped out of them, and waited, his reaction to her obvious and large in his boxers.

Afraid he might still change his mind, she kissed him, slowly, while she touched him, rubbed the head of his erection. Arousing him further. And then she was lifting her leg around his waist, trying to wrap herself around him. She wanted him. Now. Hard. Fast. Satisfying.

Raphael moved, took her around the waist, lifted her into his arms and charged upstairs to his bedroom, his manhood knocking against her butt.

What was wrong with where they were? She didn't ask. With her finger she teased his nipple, made it peak and him cry out. Then they were on the bed and she was tugging her panties off and tossing them aside. Raphael pulled her dress up to her waist and bent down to lick her.

'No. Now. You, me, together.'

He quickly sheathed himself, then rose above her and thrust into her. Hard and fast. She cried out and pushed up towards him to take him again.

It was over almost before they started. She'd been desperate to make love to him. To show him how she felt.

Isabella fell back against the pillow, her breast rising and falling rapidly.

Raphael sprawled out beside her, and draped an arm over her waist.

'Rafe.'

'Shh…don't say anything.'

She stared up at the ceiling, seeing nothing in the dark. He didn't want to talk. *She* wanted to tell him she loved him, but the words kept getting stuck in her throat. She still didn't quite trust herself to be one hundred per cent certain she loved him, and at the same time she did. That was the trouble. She knew, bone deep, he was the only man for her. But she still needed to know that these feelings weren't about settling down and making the life she'd craved since she was a kid. She'd done it once, had truly believed it was right, that her love had been for Darren and not just that picture, and she couldn't have been more wrong.

Raphael listened to Izzy's breathing as she slowly got her breath back. Did that really just happen? She'd been like a wildcat, taking him without preamble, turning him on so fast he'd hardly kept up. He'd tried to slow down, but she wasn't having it.

Hell, he'd tried to avoid going to bed with her altogether. After seeing the sadness lurking in her eyes as she witnessed her friend's betrothal he'd known he had to stop leading her on. Not that he was deliberately playing with her, but he didn't think he could promise her what she so desperately wanted—a for ever love, marriage and children. Yes, he had been moving on from Cassie a lot faster now, and believed she was history. She'd left him, and that was that.

As for Joshua, he had a way to go on that, and probably would never completely get over the pain. But before he could move forward he had to tell Isabella, and then his family.

And he just wasn't sure how to do it. It meant exposing his heart, his vulnerabilities. Izzy knew him well, but still. It wasn't easy. He'd never talked much about the things that mattered, had kept them in wrappers so no one could use them against him.

Tell her now.

She wasn't sleeping. Her breathing had returned to normal, wide awake normal. He opened his mouth. Closed it. No. Not yet. He rolled away, stretched the length of the bed and prepared to wait the night out.

At last Raphael's breathing deepened.

Isabella carefully slid out of bed and crept out of the room. In the bathroom she took a short shower, then dressed in track pants and a sweatshirt before heading downstairs where the crossword book lay on the bench. She was done with trying to sleep, and with thinking about her and Raphael. There were no answers at the moment.

The sky was beginning to lighten and the birds were waking up, chirping happily, lucky things. Her body ached. Her heart was heavy.

Her head pounded. Despite the number of times she'd not known what to do with her life, she'd never felt quite this bad.

A phone began ringing. Raphael's tune. Looking around, she couldn't see it. Listening harder, she followed the sound out to the hallway and his jacket. As she removed it from the pocket the ringing stopped.

At least it won't be work, she thought.

It rang again.

Raphael's mother's name showed on the screen.

'*Bonjour*, this is Isabella.'

'Is Raphael there?' Celeste sounded stressed.

'He's up in his bedroom. Hold on, and I'll run up there.'

'Izzy? Who is it?' Raphael appeared at the top of the stairs.

'Your mother.'

He jogged down and took the phone. 'Maman, what's happened?'

Izzy held her breath as she blatantly listened to Rafe's side of the conversation.

'When did that happen? During the night?' Rafe looked to her and held the phone away from his ear. 'Grand'mère's in hospital. Fell down the stairs. Again.' He put the phone back to his ear. 'Maman, what are her injuries? Are they serious?'

Izzy reached for his free hand and gripped it. 'Is she going to be all right?' Grateful she understood French, Izzy stayed still, and waited. Fingers crossed nothing too serious had happened.

'She broke her other hip? And her femur?' Raphael looked shocked. 'And she's unconscious?'

This did not sound good. Raphael had to go home and see his grandmother, as soon as possible. Isabella headed for the kitchen and her phone, tugging Raphael along with her. Typing in London to Avignon on her airline app, she waited for the flights to come up.

'Being in a coma is worse than broken bones.' Raphael shoved a hand through his thick hair, his gaze clouded with worry. '*Oui.* I'll come as soon as I can. Yes, today if possible.'

Isabella tapped his shoulder, said, 'There's a flight at 5:45 out of Heathrow.'

He raised his thumb. 'Maman, Izzy's on to it already. I'll send the details as soon as I have them.' His phone clattered onto the bench. He did the fingers through his hair thing again, while reaching out to her with his other hand. 'You heard? She's in a coma after falling down the stairs going down to her room, which she's not meant to be using yet. Stubborn old lady.'

'I know those steps. None too forgiving for old bones. Or her head.' Grand'mère was strong but still. Who knew what the outcome would be?

'I need to see for myself, find out all the details from the doctors. Let me look at that flight.' Moments later, 'Yes, I'll take it. But I'd better talk to someone on the ward first, make sure they can cover for me for a couple of days at least. Not that I'm not going to Avignon.'

'You do that while I fill in your details here.' She paused, drew a breath. Now was not the time to be sulking over their relationship. 'Would you like me to come with you?'

He hesitated, locking his eyes with hers,

then nodded. 'Yes. I would, very much. *Merci beaucoup*, Izzy.'

Raphael stood staring out the window, his shoulders tight, his back straight, as he talked to two different specialists about his patients. 'Thanks, Jerome. I'll call as soon as I know what's what over there. Won't be until tomorrow though, as I don't touch down until somewhere around ten tonight.'

'You wouldn't have your passport number on your phone by any chance?' Isabella asked as soon as he'd finished his calls.

Tap, tap. 'Here. And here's my bank card. Thanks, Izzy. You're a champ.' He was rubbing her neck as he watched over her shoulder as she finalised their bookings for one-way flights. 'Sorry about this.'

'Hey.' She twisted around on the stool. 'Don't apologise.' This could be good for them. Time together dealing with Grand'mère's accident and learning what the consequences would be. Serious compared to fun. Real life. And she'd be able to see for herself how determined he was to return to Avignon in the future, because not even Raphael would be able to hide the longing if it was what he wanted.

Leaning over, he brushed his lips across her brow. 'You're sure you don't mind coming?'

'Absolutely. That's what friends are for.'

He stared at her. 'Of course.' Then he turned away. 'I'll go and pack.'

CHAPTER NINE

'OH, GRAND'MÈRE, LOOK at you,' Rafe croaked around a throat full of tears the next day. 'Is she going to be all right?' he asked the hovering consultant.

Isabella reached for his hand, and held tight. She might be a nurse, but the sight of his grandmother's colourless face and her long, dark grey hair a knotted mess on the white pillow had shocked her.

'What to say? She's in a coma. Sadly.' The older man lifted a shoulder. 'There've been no signs of her coming out of it yet.'

'What about the fractures?' Raphael and the consultant got into a discussion about injuries and treatment.

Izzy extracted her hand and leaned over the rail that had been put up around the bed in case Grand'mère managed to move and fall off the bed. She reached for one of the cold, thin and wrinkled hands on top of the sheet. 'Hello, Grand'mère. It's Isabella.' Her heart sank. This accident could change Grand'mère's life for ever. But that was getting ahead of things. 'I haven't seen you for years. Raphael and I were talking about coming to see you as soon as we both had the same days off from the ward, but seems you beat us to it, got us hurrying across.'

Not a blink. No movement. The hand lay limp in hers. She rubbed her thumb back and forth over the cold skin on the back of Grand'mère's hand.

Rafe's hand gripped her shoulder. 'I'm staying here for a while. I don't want to leave her on her own. Silly, I know, but I can't help it.'

'Rafe, it's okay. You're only feeling what most people do in these situations. Useless, and worried. Your doctor hat is no help to you in this case. In fact, it's worse because you know all the things that can go wrong.' He'd have a mental list scrolling through his mind non-stop.

'Don't pull any punches, will you?' he

grunted. 'But you're right. I'm a doctor with no role to play here.'

'Yes, you do. Grand'mère will want you giving her cheek and telling her to hurry and wake up. That's your job here. We can go back to the house for some sleep later.' They'd got very little last night by the time they'd landed in Avignon and then sat up talking with his parents. Nor had they the previous night, trying out that bed in various ways. At least when she went to bed to sleep she did actually sleep now. Had been since the first night with Rafe. It gave her a sense of knowing she was doing the right thing by staying with him, and believing they could make a go of this.

'Couldn't get two more different nights if I tried.' Seemed he could still read her mind even when distressed. Better remember that.

She glanced up at him. 'Know which one I'd prefer.'

Some of the gloom had lifted and he sounded a little more relaxed. 'Me too. Thanks for being here. It means everything. I don't feel so alone.'

Raphael wasn't alone. There was a large family in the city and surrounds. 'Don't get all sentimental on me, Rafe, or I'll have to paint your bedroom orange when I get back to London.' His least favourite colour by a long shot.

'Ha. When you've finished there you could come over here and do up the family house. Despite everything going on, I couldn't help but notice how tired and dated it is, and instantly I was thinking you would turn this into something special.'

Except I live in London. Not Avignon.

'What? Because I painted one hall, I'm a decorator extraordinaire now?' Was this where his thoughts were heading? Was he already considering moving back now that his grandmother might need him? Where would that leave her? Back in London where she had stated categorically her intention of living permanently, or moving to France on yet another attempt to stop and settle down? *Whoa. Slow down.* Just like the long-term future plans, she hadn't started on settling into her flat yet.

And don't forget you wanted to know what his thoughts were on moving.

'I've never seen her looking so frail and old, Izzy. It's a reality check. She's getting older by the week.'

Nothing to say to that, so Isabella reached for his hand again and held him.

'Even once she's out of the coma, it's going to take time and patience for her to get back on her feet. I'm not sure how well she'll cope either. Her bones are fragile, and healing takes so much longer at eighty-five.'

He wasn't even considering she might not regain consciousness. Isabella liked his determined positivity. 'Nor is she known for her patience.'

'True. But what worries me most is that her confidence will have been knocked badly. I've seen it happen often enough in the elderly to expect it, but this is Grand'mère. You know what I mean?'

'Yes, Rafe, I do. She's special to you, and this is the last thing you want for her.' He'd have pictured her always being there in his life, even when that wasn't possible. *'I'm*

SUE MACKAY

247

struggling with the idea of her not getting around, bossing everyone she meets, while listening to people when they needed an ear to bend.'

'It'll be a role reversal. Strange, but only a few weeks ago she was telling me that if anything happened to her she did not want to go into a rest home. Apparently those are for old people.'

'I'm surprised she was even thinking about it. Like she'd had a premonition.' Grand'mère was a person who knew exactly what she wanted and did everything to make it happen. 'Did she say where she'd like to go?'

'She'll stay downstairs as previous generations have, and if necessary we can employ full-time care, though that won't be fun for the nurses.'

'I see.'

They pulled up chairs and sat with his grandmother for another hour when Raphael suddenly stood up and stretched. 'Let's go for a walk through the city.'

'Some fresh air would be good.' She tapped

the back of his grandmother's hand. 'We'll come back soon.'

Inside the wall the city was busy with locals and tourists crowding the streets and cafés. Isabella wandered beside Raphael, taking in the sights and scents, looking at the ancient stone walls. 'It's wonderful.'

'Coffee?' Raphael indicated a vacant table on the side of the street.

'Please. Then can we stroll through the market? I want to smell the spices.'

'I remember how you spent hours in there, buying spices that I bet you never used.' Rafe smiled and pulled out a chair for her before heading over to place their order. Then he took his phone out of his pocket and punched some numbers before wandering to the side of the café. Who was he talking to?

Isabella tried not to watch him, instead looking around at the people taking their time to walk the street, laughing, talking, pointing at buildings. Yes, she remembered that feeling of wonder the first time she visited Avignon. It was still there, making her happy when she should be worrying about

Grand'mère, but there was nothing she could do for her, so might as well make the most of time spent in the city.

When Raphael finally returned he held two cups of coffee in one hand. 'I need to stay here for a few days at least, maybe more than this week.' He cleared his throat. 'I've just talked to my colleagues and they're more than happy to cover for me for as long as I need.'

Talked to them before her? She supposed it made sense to get his priorities right. But still. 'You have to do what you feel is right for Grand'mère. After all, she's always been there for you.'

'I'm glad you understand.'

That stung. 'Why wouldn't I?' Her voice was sharper than she intended.

'Izzy. Sorry. I don't want to upset you. I know you have to go back tomorrow, and I'll miss you. You're a great support.'

'You say the nicest things when you're trying to dig yourself out of a hole, Raphael Dubois.'

'Did it work?'

As quickly as that they were back on even ground. The tension that had begun tightening her belly backed off. 'You know it did.' Being here, seeing Grand'mère, had created a new depth of understanding, sharing, helping one another. Rafe needed her to be strong and there for him. Not crashing at the first hurdle. If she got too lonely she'd get over herself, or come back here on her days off.

'Adele wants to discuss things with me tonight.'

'Things? Like what?'

'Family stuff.'

That was putting her in her place. Seemed she wasn't getting as close to him as she'd hoped. He was gazing round the area, smiling in a way she wasn't familiar with, almost as though he was at home. Guess he was. He knew these streets like the back of his hand, having spent most of his early childhood here before his family moved to Geneva.

That was what she wanted, only in London. With Raphael. Was she expecting too much? Draining her coffee, she stood up. 'I'm going to the market. I'm going to get some pastries and cheeses. Coming?'

'Yes.' He looked baffled. 'Why wouldn't I?'

She didn't have an answer. 'Tell me what I can get for your mother for tonight's dinner.' Adele wasn't the only one coming. All the Dubois family would be there.

'Maman will have everything sorted, believe me.'

'Then I'll buy flowers,' she said as they entered the Halles d'Avignon and breathed in spices and coffee and freshly baked bread.

'Leave those until we've finished wandering around or they'll be bruised from bumping into people by the time we're done in here.' There was a deep happiness in Raphael's voice that had been missing for a long time.

Isabella felt her heart drop. Not even their hot nights had brought that on so strongly. He really belonged here, and now he was starting to look around and see what he'd been missing out on all because he'd been so stubborn.

The buzz around the family dinner table later that night only increased Isabella's unease. Despite the reason for Raphael coming home everyone was laughing and talking non-stop and Rafe was right in the thick of it.

'Izzy, have some more beef. I know it's your favourite.' He didn't wait for her reply, just spooned more of the delicious stew onto her plate.

'Give her a break,' Adele laughed. 'You'll be frightening her away if you keep doing that.'

She wasn't staying long anyway. Swallowing hard, Isabella smiled and tried to relax. It wasn't easy when Raphael was enjoying himself so much. Of course she was happy for him, but with each passing hour she had to wonder if he'd ever get around to going back to London. He would. He had a job that he relished there, a home and a cat. But he belonged here too.

Raphael wound his arms around Izzy and cuddled her against his naked length as they lay in bed in his old bedroom from when he was a teen and where he stayed whenever in Avignon. It had been a bit awkward last night when they headed to bed. Maman had prepared another room for Izzy. He hadn't wanted that. He needed her with him at the moment. Selfish, maybe, but she'd come to support him, and he was grateful.

The sun was up, and he was ready to get out. 'Want to walk into the city and have breakfast by the bridge?'

She tossed the sheet aside and sat up, letting his arms slip away. 'Let's go.'

'Mind if we visit Grand'mère on the way?'

'Of course not. She's why we're here.'

Something wasn't right with Isabella, hadn't been since they arrived in Avignon on Sunday night. 'Talk to me.'

She sank her naked derriere onto the side of the bed and faced him. There was a sadness in her eyes he didn't like. 'Your family ties were strong, and couldn't be more different to mine. You are so lucky.'

Rafe nodded. 'I'm starting to think that.' Then he looked closer and felt like he'd been punched in the gut. 'You can be a part of it too, Izzy. They adore you.' Everyone had jostled for her attention last night at dinner. They'd never been like that with Cassie.

'I was made to feel special,' she admitted, still looking directly at him.

'Then what's the problem?'

'I don't know where we're going with our relationship.' She seemed to let go of some knot inside her as those words slid out of her mouth. 'Do you?'

Crunch time. He sat up fast. This wasn't how he wanted to tell her, nor where. But maybe he should just get it out of the way. Reaching for the water bottle by the bed, he tried to drink down some fluid and moisten his suddenly dry mouth, but his throat wasn't playing the game. His gut was churning. His head was banging. His heart had a whole new rhythm going on.

Izzy was watching him closely, concern filling her eyes. 'Rafe? You're frightening me.' Then she leapt up, strode across to stare out the window. 'Talk to me.'

If there was anyone he'd tell it would be Isabella. He had to tell her. She knew so much about him, what was one more thing? Ex-

cept this was huge. But if he wanted to ban-
ish that despair in her face he had no choice.
Because he just couldn't put his story away
and pretend nothing was wrong. For one, Izzy
already knew there was something wrong,
and for two, he had to be honest more than
anything. Tell Izzy. Don't tell Izzy.

'I am a father.'

Her fingers tightened around her elbows as
she turned to stare at him through wide-open
eyes, but still she said nothing.

Am a father? Was a father? What was the
protocol? Who cared? It was about his feelings. No one else's. 'Joshua. He died of SIDS
at eight days old.'

Then she moved, came and sat beside him,
reaching for his shaking hands. 'Oh, Rafe.'
His name dragged across her shaky bottom
lip. 'Raphael, I am so sorry.'

Don't show me pity. I'll fall apart.

And it would take for ever to get the pieces
back together again. 'Cassie didn't tell me she
was pregnant when she left me and returned
to Los Angeles.'

'You didn't know?' Horror filled Izzy's face.

'No. All I knew was she went back for auditions in the movie industry. She was going to become the next big name in movies. Oh, and I was a stubborn bore who wouldn't move to Paris so she could have fun in the greatest city in the world.' Not that she'd ever shown any acting aptitude when he'd known her, except to pull off huge lies. And being pregnant hadn't helped her chances of getting her first break, something she'd told him was his fault.

'I didn't find out until two years later. We hadn't communicated since she left France so I went over to see her, wanting to find closure. I couldn't wrap it up.'

'And you got the opposite,' Izzy whispered.

'I never met my son. Didn't know he existed until it was too late. Never held him, kissed him, hugged him. He didn't know I existed.' Raphael stared down at the floor. Hot tears slid down his face, dripped off his chin onto his chest. He did nothing about them. 'How could she do that to me?'

Warm arms wound around his back, tugged him close to Isabella's soft body. Her hands rubbed slow circles on his skin, her mouth brushed feather-light kisses on his neck.

'Did she hate me that much?'

'Cassie was always very selfish.'

'True. But she went beyond the realm of selfish into something so deep and hideous I can't believe it.'

Izzy tipped her head back to lock her troubled gaze with his. 'Have you talked to your family about it?'

'You're the only person I've told. I have been arguing with myself for days now over whether to say anything or to carry on as though it hadn't happened. But you deserve better than that.'

'Thank you.' With her thumb she wiped his damp cheeks. 'Is this why you've stayed away from your family?'

He nodded abruptly. 'They already disliked Cassie, they'd hate her if they knew this. And I'd always feel their wrath. It's not something they'd let go in a hurry, if at all. Also...' He breathed deep. 'I feel bad for the things she used to say about them to their faces. I made a monumental error when I fell in love with her, and I don't like seeing that in their faces every time I'm with them.'

'I think you're overreacting. Your family loves you, and that's what matters. I doubt they judge you for making a mistake. Who doesn't at some time of their life? More often than once.'

'Hell, Izzy, you're amazing. I've been dreading telling you and here you are being sensible about it all.' He really did love her, and now he'd cleared the way to follow through with that. But not now. She might think he was using her sympathy.

She leaned in to kiss him. 'Tell your parents. They'll understand.'

'It'd be cruel to tell them they were grandparents and didn't get the opportunity to be a part of Joshua's short life.' He couldn't do that to them. It was still so painful for him.

'They're tougher than you're giving them credit for, Rafe.' Izzy stood up. 'I'm going for a quick shower and then let's go see Grand'mère. You could practise on her, since she won't hear you.'

'Oh, right.' From somewhere deep inside,

he found her a smile. 'Should've told you a long time ago.'

'Yes, Rafe, you should've.'

He reached for her hands, was shocked to feel them shaking too. Anger? Sadness? Knowing Izzy, it would be a combination of a lot of emotions—all for him. 'I was afraid that if I opened up and told you I'd never be able to get myself under control again.'

'And now?'

His heart slowed, but a weight had gone from it. 'I think I'm going to make it.'

Isabella wandered through the old city centre to the Halles d'Avignon again, Raphael beside her deep in thought. Not surprising after what he'd revealed earlier. She was still trying to get her head around it. They passed people eating on the sidewalk and today her mouth didn't water as the smell of a fresh croissant and piping hot coffee reached her nose from the endless cafés.

How could Cassie have done something so cruel? Unbelievable. She'd stolen his chance of knowing his child, of knowing he had been a father. He still was a father. Along with that she'd turned him away from the very people who could've supported him through the pain and grief. Including her. He'd said he was afraid to let the pain out, for fear it would grow and spread. She understood that.

They reached the market and she hesitated. Not even the spices of every variety at the market could distract her. Glancing at Rafe she saw him smile ever so slightly, despite the heaviness on his heart. This was something he missed in London. But then he was French. And this was France. Home. He could live here all too easily. If he told his parents about Joshua. He had to. She knew that, probably better than he did, because until he did it would still be hanging over him, affecting everything he decided to do.

'Come on. I promised you breakfast and you can't back out on me now.' He leaned in to kiss her cheek.

She nodded, afraid to speak in case she told him that she understood him better than he realised, probably better than he did at the moment. He would front up to his family with the truth, and then… Yeah, and then… She couldn't put it into words. It hurt too much.

The pastry was dry on her tongue and the coffee ordinary. Finally she pushed her plate aside and watched Raphael. She loved him so much, and still couldn't find the courage to tell him.

'Come on, I'll buy you some Camembert and bleu d'Auvergne to take when you go home.'

'My favourite cheeses,' she agreed. Hopefully her appetite returned to enjoy them. 'Let's go.' Suddenly impatient to be moving she leapt up. 'I'd like to visit Grand'mère once more today.' Rafe's grandmother was still in a coma, though when they called in before coming here the doctor said she was responding a little to touch sometimes.

'I hope she has heard you talking to her. You hold a special place in her heart, as her lost Kiwi.'

Isabella felt her eyes tearing up. 'She's always been welcoming and kind to me. Even when I was a bumptious teen.'

'I think that's why she likes you. You don't take any nonsense from anyone.' Raphael's arm wrapped around her shoulders and he drew her against his side as they ducked around people to reach the cheese stall. 'Let loose, pick whatever you want.' He didn't let go of her as she chattered away to the woman behind the counter, nor when he handed over money to pay for her choices, nor as they walked back to the hospital.

She was glad, needing him, wanting him to want her.

'No change,' a nurse told them as they walked past the desk in Grand'mère's ward.

'To be expected,' Rafe said, though she could hear his despair.

'Gives you the opportunity to tell her what you don't want her to hear.'

Raphael stopped still, right in the middle of the corridor, and turned to face her. His gaze was serious and her heart lurched. She knew what was coming.

'You were right. I do need to tell the family about Joshua. I'll do it this afternoon.'

Reaching up on her toes, she brushed a kiss across his mouth. 'I'm proud of you.'

And I love you, but that's for another day.

The next morning Raphael bounced out of bed and into the shower at seven o'clock.

'Look at you, bouncing around like a kangaroo.' Izzy groaned. 'Some of us still need our sleep.'

'I had the best night in ages,' he told her. 'Slept right through. You were right. Telling Maman and Papa about Joshua was the right thing to do. I feel like a huge weight has been lifted from my heart.'

'Good. Sometimes I'm not so silly after all.'

'I'm going in to see Grand'mère and tell her, even if she is still unconscious. She'll probably wake up telling the world my story.'

'Then I'll stay here and have a lie-in.'

'See you later, then. I'll take you to the airport about two. How does that sound?'

'Awful. I don't want to go home yet.' What she really didn't want was to leave Raphael. It had been good spending time here with him, and joining his family.

'Sound like you mean it, will you?' Didn't he want her to go either?

She laughed. 'Say hello to Grand'mère for me.'

An hour later she rolled out of bed and into the shower before going to make a coffee and sit on the terrace overlooking the edge of the city and the Rhône beyond. It was beautiful with all the stonework and the wall that surrounded the city. But it wasn't home. That was London. She had to keep believing that or she'd be back at the beginning, not knowing where she was headed.

'Morning, Isabella.' Raphael's mother stepped onto the deck, a cup of coffee in hand. 'Beautiful morning, *oui*?'

'Stunning.'

'Where's Raphael?'

'He's gone into the hospital to see Grand'-mère.'

'I can't believe what that woman did to him.' Celeste sat down beside her. 'It is cruel. He'll always wonder what his boy looked like.'

'Yes, he will.' It was the most hideous thing someone could do, and Cassie had once loved Raphael. Had that not counted for anything?

'It's good that he told us. We can understand why he's stayed away now. Not that he should've. We'd always support him.'

'I think he knows that.'

Celeste sipped her coffee and stared out over the balustrade. 'And what about you, Isabella? You're settling into London?'

'Yes, I am. I can't wait to move into my flat and start putting my own mark on it.'

'How long do you think you'll be there?'

Hello? What was this about? 'Long term.'

'I see.'

Isabella's stomach cramped. What did she see? 'Do you? It's been a long time since I've stopped in one place, and never for ever. I need to do this.'

'What about Raphael?'

'What about him?' The cramps turned to hard squeezing. Her heart began racing.

'He belongs here, Isabella. With his family. He misses Avignon and all of us, especially Grand'mère.'

She couldn't argue with that. 'He does.'

Now Celeste turned to face her. 'Thank you for understanding.' Then she got up and headed inside.

Leaving Isabella stunned. Of course his family would want him to return home. Face it, so did Raphael. It was her who had to either change her mind about where she'd live or give up on any thoughts of getting together with Rafe. Not that he was actively encouraging them. She was hanging her hope on the fact he hadn't stopped having sex with her. It had to mean something, didn't it? Or was she being naïve?

Damn it. She couldn't sit around here waiting for him to return from the hospital. She'd go for a walk.

But not even the stunning views of the river and city from the old fort could distract her. She felt as though she was walking in quicksand, getting deeper and deeper without any sign of a way out. She'd fallen for Raphael so hard she literally didn't know what to do with herself. To give up her own goals to follow him wherever he chose to live would be easier than fighting for what she wanted. But giving up her own dreams after finally starting to realise them was not being true to herself. But hey, she was getting way ahead of herself. He wasn't exactly reciprocating her love.

When Raphael stepped through the front door he heard voices coming from the lounge and headed towards them.

'Raphael, you remember Louis Fournier? From the hospital,' Papa said as he entered the room.

He put his hand out to shake the older man's. *'Bonjour, Docteur.'* From the smug look on his face, Papa was up to something. 'It's been a while since I talked to you.'

'It has. I've been keeping up with your career through your father though. You've done well.'

'Thank you. I've worked hard to get where I am, for sure. So what brings you out here?'

'Louis has some news for you.'

'I see,' said Rafe. But he didn't. Though he was beginning to suspect where this might be heading. 'Let's sit out in the conservatory.' There he'd be able to look out over the houses and the fort as he listened to what this man was about to say. He'd be able to see his hometown and think about a future here, compare it to what he had in London.

'I'll come straight to the point,' Louis said. 'There's a position for a gynaecologist coming up at the general hospital. I wondered if you might be interested.'

'Yes, definitely.' His heart rate sped up. Of course he was. His lifelong dream to practise medicine here was falling into place.

Izzy.

He couldn't walk away from her now. It was the only thing he was certain about. She'd been the one to convince him to talk about Joshua to his family. She'd come here with him when he was so worried about Grand'mère. She wasn't Cassie. He'd have to convince her she could start over—again—when he'd spent the last few weeks helping her realise she was where she really wanted to be. No, he couldn't do that to her.

Raphael closed his eyes, breathed deep, searching for answers. Found none. Or far too many. Look out for Izzy, the love of his heart? Or follow his own dreams and hope she'd tag along? No. He'd never ask that of her. Nor did he want to give up this opportunity in Avignon where his family was. For the first time in years he was ready to live where he belonged. If he could figure out a way to keep everyone happy.

'So? What do you think?' Papa was back. 'Couldn't be better timing, eh?'

Oh, yes, it could. Damn it. He wanted to take it up. Desperately. *So do it.* Inside, his heart was cracking. Half for Izzy, half for Avignon. This couldn't be happening. But it was. Yet he'd never felt quite so strongly about returning here until now. Grand'mère's accident had brought home to him that if he was to spend time with his family, now was it. 'How soon do you need a decision?'

'Why don't we go in now and I can show you around, introduce you to our team, give you a general idea of how we run things here?' Obviously Louis had no intention of letting him make up his mind slowly. At least, not without all barrels being fired first.

What did he have to lose? Though he already thought he knew his answer. He wasn't destined to fly solo when his heart belonged to Isabella. 'Sure. As long as I'm back in time to take Isabella to the airport.'

Isabella watched Raphael change into a suit and comb his hair. 'Something you want to tell me?'

'I'm popping out but I should be back in time to take you to the airport. If not, Maman will give you a lift.'

'You're going to the hospital to look at an opportunity of a position there.'

He stared at her as though she'd done something wrong.

'If you didn't want me to hear your conversation with Monsieur Fournier, then you should've stayed away from our bedroom window.'

He winced.

Her hands gripped her hips. 'So, Raphael, are you planning to move back here? Taking this job?'

'No... Yes... I don't know.'

'I see.' She didn't really. But she was angry. 'Thanks for not telling me about any of this. Was I supposed to wait and accept whatever you chose to do without hesitation? I know we've agreed to take our time working out where our relationship might lead, but not being open with me isn't going to help.'

'Izzy, we'll talk on the way to the airport.'

'No, thanks. I'll find my own way there. You go and see what's on offer at the hospital.' She turned her back on him and waited for him to leave the room.

'Isabella, I am sorry. I do need to make some decisions. I just don't know what they'll be.'

Less than an hour later Isabella paid off the taxi, slung her bag over her shoulder and went to check in. Her heart was numb.

Raphael had been offered a position at the hospital in Avignon. She should've expected it. He'd take it up. When asked by Monsieur Fourier if he might be interested he'd said, 'Yes, definitely.'

She boarded her flight and sank into her

seat, closed her eyes and pretended to be asleep.

For the first time since meeting Raphael she wanted to hate him. He'd lied by omission. They were better than that. He should have told her the truth. But instead of hating him, she loved him.

Which hurt like hell.

CHAPTER TEN

THE EXPECTANT MOTHER who'd been admitted an hour ago with early contractions was reading a book and quite comfortable with her lot—for now. Isabella's heart hadn't been in her work all day so when sign-off time came around she was out of the ward like a rabbit being chased by a hound.

Once she finally staggered into Raphael's house, exhausted from lack of sleep, she headed for the fridge and the wine, rubbing the small of her back where a persistent ache had started up hours ago. 'What a day. It couldn't have got any slower if it tried.'

Taking her glass with her, she wandered outside to the deck and slumped into the first chair. Chienne was quick to jump and spread herself across Izzy's thighs. 'Hey, you. Lonely too?'

Purr, purr.

'Okay, so you'll settle for anyone as long as you have food and cuddles.' Next week she'd be moving into the apartment she'd rented and beginning to unpack the mountain of kitchenware and other things she'd bought. It would be the start of everything she'd hoped for. Except a life with Raphael. He wouldn't leave his house to move into a tiny one-bed apartment. But he might—make that probably would—leave this place for Avignon and the family he'd started getting back with.

A sharp breeze skipped across the yard, lifting leaves and chilling her skin. 'Guess we're going inside, Chienne. Wasn't enjoying it that much out here anyway.'

After making sure she was locked in, Isabella headed upstairs, not to Raphael's bedroom but to the third floor where she crawled under the covers on the bed, still in her clothes. Who cared? The cat followed, and quickly made herself comfortable curled up against Isabella's leg. Looking around, she sighed. The room she'd used for the first weeks was cold and uninviting, the bed not welcoming. No hints of Rafe. There again, not even his bedroom had been warm and inviting when she'd popped her head in earlier.

'At the end of the day, without Raphael this place is only a house, not a home.' She blinked hard. 'I love him.' So much it was unbearable. Did she really want to give him up to live in a one-bed downstairs apartment? After seeing Raphael's enjoyment as he wandered around Avignon the idea of living in London so she could have her own home was turning cold. What was the point if she wasn't with the love of her life? An old saying slipped into her head. 'Home is where the heart is.'

It was like someone had turned the lights on. Blink, blink. She couldn't leave Raphael. She'd go to the end of the earth if it meant being with him. And yes, she'd travel to different countries, other cities, if she had to. Though that was unlikely. If they settled in Avignon, it would be for a long time, probably for ever. She could do this. And be happy about it. She was in love. Nothing could be better than that. Could it? No, it couldn't.

* * *

From the hospital Raphael went into the city centre for a look around. He rolled his shoulders as he walked, trying to ease the tightness brought on by the dismay in Isabella's eyes as she told him he hadn't been honest with her. He breathed in the scent of the place, recalling other times he'd been here, with Grand'mère, his parents, his cousins. He knew most corners and streets, not much had changed. It was familiar in a comfortable way. Old yet pulsing with new energy. Tourists and locals alike sitting outside cafés enjoying the sun and coffee.

As he passed a bar the sounds of a rugby game on the television reached him and he paused to look in. The French were playing the Italians. If it had been the All Blacks playing Izzy might've been watching.

His heart lurched. She'd gone. In anger. And pain. He'd let her down. Badly. It was time to tell her how he felt.

Which was why he was walking around his beloved city, taking in everything, storing up new memories.

He tugged his phone out of his back pocket and pressed her number.

'Raphael.' Her voice was flat.

'Izzy, I'm sorry.'

'Sure.'

Right. 'Can you pick me up from Heathrow tonight?'

'You're returning home?'

What she was really asking was, *Are you coming home for good?* 'Of course I am.' Except there was no of course about it. In reply to her question about if he was moving home he'd answered no and yes. Home was a new word for him. It wasn't just a house with a bed in it any more. It was where his heart lay. Except his heart had been torn. London and Avignon. Izzy and his family. Would it have been greedy to want it all?

'Okay.'

He tried another tack. 'Grand'mère opened her eyes for a few minutes this afternoon.' It should've been the first thing he told Izzy, but he'd been overwhelmed with his love of his city and had to say something about it before it consumed him. Telling Izzy his dilemma should be a priority, but he was afraid to put it out there until he knew for sure what he would do. 'I was doing my talking thing, chatting about anything and everything, and looked over and there she was staring at me.' His heart had gone into overdrive as he'd reached for her wrist to check her pulse.

'Hey, that's great news.' Finally some enthusiasm. 'Give her another hug from me.'

'Already did.'

'What time do you get in?' Flat again.

He told her the fight number and arrival time. 'I'll see you later.'

'Okay.'

Who knew if she'd turn up to collect him, but he had to believe she would. Tossing the phone on the bed, he quickly shoved his clothes into the bag, for once not folding anything. He had a flight to catch and missing it was not an option.

His phone pinged as he paced the terminal, waiting to board his flight.

Get it right, my boy.

Grand'mère. Nothing wrong with her brain after the coma.

His gut churned. What if Isabella turned her back on him? What if she'd decided he wasn't worth the effort? Only one way to find out, and he had to endure two flights first.

Both flights were slower than a winter's day. At Heathrow Customs it took for ever just to reach the grumpy-looking woman behind the desk.

His phone pinged as he handed over his passport. Izzy.

I'm here.

'Excuse me, sir. I'm asking you to turn that off while you're here.' The grumpy official dragged out the questions like he was an illegal alien trying to get across the border. Finally his passport was approved and he was free to go.

Striding out into the arrivals hall he scanned the crowd, missed Izzy the first time. Then on a second sweep he saw her standing to one side, tired and sad. No human tornado tonight. His heart squeezed. 'Izzy,' he called as he crossed to stand in front of her. When he reached to hug her she stepped back.

'Did you take the job?'

'No. I didn't.'

'Why didn't you tell me that's what you were going into town for?'

Dropping his bag to the floor, he laid both hands on her shoulders. 'Because I didn't want to upset you when I had no idea if I'd take it or not. I wanted to be certain one way or the other before saying anything.'

She stared at him, her eyes wide and filled with a pain he'd never seen there before. 'Really?'

'Really. Really didn't know. And really turned it down. I live in London, Izzy.'

She blinked, bit her lip.

'I've come home to tell you I'm not moving away, that Avignon's a part of me but not all of me. I've finally come to my senses and see that returning there was a dream, and now that the opportunity has arisen to live and work there, it all feels wrong. I won't deny a part of my heart will always be there with my family, but…' He drew a breath. This was the moment he had to put himself out there. 'But really, my heart belongs with you. In London, in our house. I love you, Izzy.'

'Rafe? You do?' A tear snuck from the corner of her eye.

'Yes. I love you, Isabella Nicholson, with everything I have.'

'I love you, too,' she whispered. Then louder, 'I love you, Rafe, and it's been so hard thinking you wouldn't love me back.'

'Oh, Izzy.' He wrapped his arms around her familiar body and held on tight.

'I can't believe us.'

'Right pair, aren't we? Great friends, awesome lovers, and now for the future.' He pulled back enough to gaze down into her eyes, and he knew he couldn't wait until they got home. He dug into his pocket for the small box he'd put there hours ago, and dropped to one knee. 'Isabella Nicholson, will you do the honour of marrying me?'

She gasped. 'Raphael? Did I hear what I think I did?'

'Please marry me, Izzy? I love you so

much I can't bear the thought of not being with you.'

She went quiet on him again, but he wasn't worried. She wouldn't have lied about loving him. Just being typical Izzy, making him wait. 'Answer the question, will you, Izzy?' he pleaded.

Then her sweet, fierce voice whispered, 'I love you, Rafe, more than anything, but I am not asking you to give up your dreams for me.'

'I'm not. Yes, I adore my family and being back in Avignon has been wonderful, but I mean it. My heart is with you in London.'

'I can live anywhere if we're together,' she said. 'Yes, Rafe, I will marry you. Till death do us part in about sixty years' time.'

Phew. She was smiling right at him. Hadn't realised he was holding his breath.

'Are we seriously engaged?'

He slid Grand'mère's engagement ring onto her finger. 'As of now, yes.'

'Mummy, what's that man doing?'

'Asking the pretty lady to marry him.'

'Why?'

Raphael looked across to the little boy staring at him. 'Because I love this lady and want to be with her for the rest of my life.'

Loud cheers and lots of clapping drowned out anything else the child might have said. Raphael swung Izzy up in his arms and kissed her before he turned for the exit.

'Hey, mister, you've forgotten your bag.' A man ran after them, a silly grin on his face.

'Thanks.' He grinned back, happy as a man could get.

But at the car, his Isabella stood swinging the keys in her hand and looking slightly bemused. 'I can't promise you I'll settle easily, though I know it's you I want in my life more than a home in one place. If we move house every year I will be happy. And I certainly won't object to moving across to Avignon to be a part of your family.'

'*You* are my family, Izzy. I've got a home that as of now is ours. We both have jobs we love, though I'm going to look for something less time-consuming so I can have more time with you. There are our friends nearby we like to spend time with. We have everything that matters.'

A sob came across the rooftop of the car. 'You say the nicest things when you're not trying to annoy me.'

'Love you, sweetheart.'

EPILOGUE

Months later

HARRY TAPPED HIS glass with a knife from the dining table. 'Okay, everyone, please raise your glasses for a toast to the disgustingly happy couple.'

Isabella reached for Rafe's hand, and entwined her fingers between his. 'We did it.' It had taken time to organise a dinner in their London home with their friends. Everyone was so busy and a baby had been born, but eventually they'd managed it. If only they could get married now, but divorces took time, and she had to be patient.

'If you're half as happy as Esther and I, then well done.' Harry held his glass before him.

Raphael grinned. 'I reckon.'

'Cheers,' everyone shouted, before drinking to them.

Isabella felt the tears burning lines down her face, and grinned. They were happy tears. 'Thanks, everyone. I'm just glad we've joined you all in wedded bliss, or in our case, on the way to marriage.' This was the bliss, the wedded component to follow when she was single again. 'Less than nine months to go before the big day.'

At that, Raphael glanced at her, a question in his eye.

She nodded. They'd agreed about this before everyone got here.

His hand squeezed hers before he announced, 'We're going to join some of you in the parenting stakes too.'

The room erupted and Isabella found herself wrapped in Carly's arms. 'Go, girlfriend. That's awesome news.'

'Who'd have thought?'

'Everyone but you.' Carly smiled, and turned to Adem to scoop her daughter out of his arms and against her swollen breasts.

'She's gorgeous.' Izzy smiled.

'Here, have a hold. Derya Ann, this is your godmother.'

Izzy's heart swelled further as she took the warm bundle. 'She's so beautiful.' She sniffed. 'I'm so happy it's scary.'

'Not scary. Wonderful.' Carly grinned. 'Now, can I have my daughter back?'

Harry did his spoon-tapping-glass thing again. His smile was wider and softer as he focused on Esther, nothing but love in his eyes. 'We, too, are pregnant.' Once again the room exploded with joy and laughter and shouts.

Then Esther and Chloe were nudging Carly aside to give Isabella a hug. 'Go, you. A baby. No wonder you're looking so peachy.'

Peachy? Yuck. Isabella grinned and flapped her hand. 'I'm so glad Rafe suggested I come back to London.'

'The man had an ulterior motive,' Xander said.

'It worked, didn't it?' Rafe said.

Yes, it had. And she couldn't be happier. She had found her match, the man to go through life with, raise children with, laugh and love and do all the things she'd been hoping for. It didn't matter where, only that she was with Rafe. She took one more sip of her champagne and put the glass down. From now on water would suffice until their wedding day by which time junior would've put in an appearance.

Life couldn't be better.

* * * * *